PUFFIN BOOKS

DOG DAYS AND CAT NAPS

In this delightful collection of short stories animals play a
prominent part, though not to the exclusion of their human
owners, friends and slaves. Cats (ranging from the mysteri-
ously powerful to the frankly inept) make many appear-
ances, as do gerbils and assorted dogs, including Crasher,
whose heavy-footed approach to life provides a title for the
final story.

Six of the ten stories are told by the children who take part
in them, and most of the stories are funny. But there is sad-
ness too (in *Joe's Cat*) and eeriness (in *The Plagues*, where
Simon discovers the frightening consequences of showing
disrespect to an ancient monument).

Other books by Gene Kemp

CHARLIE LEWIS PLAYS FOR TIME
THE CLOCK TOWER GHOST
GOWIE CORBY PLAYS CHICKEN
THE TURBULENT TERM OF TYKE TILER
JASON BODGER AND THE PRIORY GHOST
JUNIPER
JUST FERRET
THE WELL
DUCKS AND DRAGONS (ed.)

For older readers

I CAN'T STAND LOSING
NO PLACE LIKE

Gene Kemp

Dog Days
and Cat Naps

Illustrated by Carolyn Dinan

PUFFIN BOOKS
in association with Faber and Faber

PUFFIN BOOKS

Published by the Penguin Group
Penguin Books Ltd, 27 Wrights Lane, London W8 5TZ, England
Penguin Books USA Inc., 375 Hudson Street, New York, New York 10014, USA
Penguin Books Australia Ltd, Ringwood, Victoria, Australia
Penguin Books Canada Ltd, 10 Alcorn Avenue, Toronto, Ontario, Canada M4V 3B2
Penguin Books (NZ) Ltd, 182–190 Wairau Road, Auckland 10, New Zealand

Penguin Books Ltd, Registered Offices: Harmondsworth, Middlesex, England

First published by Faber and Faber Ltd, 1980
Published in Puffin Books 1983
7 9 10 8

Printed in England by Clays Ltd, St Ives plc
Set in Baskerville

Contents

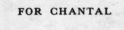
FOR CHANTAL

The Grey Invader

During the war, I lived in a small village in the heart of England. We had two cats, but no dog, as my mother would not have dogs. I loved these cats dearly—John, an elderly bachelor of a cat with quiet ways and a wavy tail, and Patsy, a black cat with white paws, white whiskers and a white stomach, very dainty and intelligent, one of the most intelligent animals I've known. She could steal groceries out of bicycle baskets, open pantry and cupboard doors to track down meat, scoop goldfish out of bowls, and, after a hunting spree in the fields, would line up her little dormice and vole victims exactly in order of size, the longest first, in the porch, to greet whoever was coming in. A mathematical cat, perhaps? She also caught rabbits, and, later on, when food rationing grew tight, my mother would cook these rabbits, though she did not tell us at the time in case it put us off. I can remember my brother scoffing rabbit pie with relish, then suddenly looking round the table and exclaiming in a horrified voice, for five of the family were eating rabbit legs with fingers and gusto, especially my father, never a dainty eater—

"We're eating a deformed rabbit! It's got five legs!"

"No, dear," answered my mother placidly. "There are two rabbits."

I knew where she'd got the second one from, because I'd been there when Patsy had carried it home in triumph. But we didn't tell.

Patsy had two other unusual qualities. She ate peas, which I've never seen another cat do, and she used to go wild with delight when we shelled them, chasing those that dropped on the floor, making them roll about like marbles. Her other peculiarity was this. That cat loved my brother better than anyone else, although she was given to me in the first place. When he went into the army, she missed him, as we all did, and as much, I think, as cats ever miss anyone, for they are lovers of places rather than people. Well, Patsy always knew when he was coming on leave, sometimes when we didn't. She would suddenly run up our lane to the village green, and sit there, and sure enough, quite soon, my brother would appear, walking up the hill and round the corner towards home. And the little cat—she never grew very big—would accompany him home in triumph, purring and rubbing round his legs.

As well as our cats, there were catty neighbours. Next door to us, but some distance away, the houses in the lane being rather spread out, lived a middle-aged lady, tall and timid, with ingrowing eyelashes, very painful, that fascinated me. She lived in a grand house, one up, or even nine or ten up, on ours, and she had a big, stout tabby cat. Next door to us on the other side was an extremely beautiful, long-haired black cat, who was always giving birth to kittens; that's how I'd had

10

Patsy in the first instance, for she was one of them. But Patsy herself, though seven years old by now, had never had any kittens, and since one year of a cat's life equals seven of ours, this made her forty-nine, so I reckoned if she was going to have some gorgeous, lovely, marvellous baby kittens, she'd better get a move on. I was a bit tired of waiting. There were never enough animals, you see. I always wanted more.

Miss Telfer, the lady with the funny eyelashes, was a nervous lady, living alone. We were under threat of invasion, expecting the Germans to land any day. Our village organised parachute-spotting from a high field in the area. You couldn't call it a hill, for they don't go in for hills much in that part of the Midlands, but sitting in the parachute-spotter's hut you could see for many miles, as far as the spires of Lichfield Cathedral, known as the Ladies of the Vale. All the fields were filled with the trunks of trees which had been cut down and scattered around to stop planes landing easily. Once a week, I went parachute-spotting with my friend, and, deep inside, I wondered what I should actually *do* if I saw a plane landing or enemy parachutes streaming down from the wild blue yonder. We had our orders abut phoning, etc., but as I sat with my friend Ethel, chewing gum and reading comics, I didn't feel we were up to much as Defenders of the Village.

Now, all this atmosphere of invasion began to upset Miss Telfer, living alone as she did, and from time to time, she flipped her lid, as we called it, and would shoot out of her house, rush up the village street—there was only one, with two or three lanes leading off it—and back down again, crying at the top of her voice (like

Cassandra, that batty Greek lady, who spent her time telling everybody that dreadful things were going to happen, and nobody believing her):

"The Germans have landed!"

or sometimes:

"The Russians have landed!"

depending on how she felt at the time.

She was a very tall lady, as I've said, and her long legs flapped like herons, as she ran up and back again, warning us of our doom. Not that we ever did anything, as no one believed her, and even if we had, just what were we supposed to do? Somebody, often my mother, would make her a cup of tea, and take her back home again, till next time.

One day, as I sat with my cronies on the pavement outside the village shop, racking our brains to find a money-raising scheme, Miss Telfer bounded up the street and it was the Germans again. We didn't take much notice, for what we were all staring at was right behind her, where stalked the most magnificent and triumphant-looking cat I have ever seen from that day to this. His thick coat varied from pearl grey to deepest blue, his eyes were jade green, his tail, wide as a cricket bat, stuck jauntily in the air, and his ears were proud and alert. Up the street he walked like a pirate, every-one watching. Jack Archer's dog, the one said to be mad, came out and barked at him. The cat checked for a moment, spat, and then continued in the bright

sunshine. Jack Archer's dog, the fiercest in the village, ran away, tail down.

"Whose cat is it?" hissed Winnie Archer. "Our dog never runs away."

No one knew who he was or where he came from and we never found out.

He moved in first with Miss Telfer and the stout tabby. After that, he made his way round the village, sleeping where he liked, eating what he pleased. And he ate and slept well, everyone going out of their way to look after him, as if it were an honour, for he had such an air about him, such presence, as though he were a fairy-tale prince or a magician in disguise.

Time passed. We waited to be invaded. All over the country the skies were busy with warfare, and we listened to the radio every day. The weather grew lovelier and lovelier, the leaves thick and green, and home-made ice-cream was greatly in demand. The grey cat continued visiting. He came late to us, by which time I was a bit jealous. He moved into our shed. John, the old bachelor cat, spat bitterly once, then retired to live in a bush beside our well, only coming out to eat, and sulking steadily. Patsy purred and rolled herself on the lawn, flashing her white tum. The great cat prowled the garden in his grey-and-blue striped fur.

The weather grew even hotter, if possible. Miss Telfer flipped her lid several times, and other people muttered darkly that they would do the same if such news and the weather continued.

Every day the grey cat patrolled up and down the village street. But now, small gatherings of the village toms were to be found watching from doorways, alley-ways, roof-tops, apparently ignoring him, but always there, always watching, watching.

The storm arrived, at last, in the middle of the night. So bad was it, that we all got up and sat downstairs, me on my father's knee, the place the lightning would be least likely to strike, I thought. My mother had all the windows and doors wide open, for she had the idea that if a thunderbolt came down the chimney it had to have somewhere to get out again or the house would explode, which seemed sensible enough, except that it was jolly uncomfy sitting there in the middle of the night, in the dark (for we had to have the lights off as well, in case our electricity attracted the storm's electricity) and with everything flapping because of the violent gale and storm raging overhead. It roared away for a long time, and next day it was discovered that the church tower had been hit, the cricket pavilion lifted clean over a hedge and smashed, and, wait for it, a thunderbolt had fallen in the circle of trees in the field next to our house.

"I told you, Albert," my mother said to my dad.

Those trees were never the same again.

There was also another casualty.

In the middle of that circle of trees, though not burned or marked in any way by the storm, lay the grey cat, quite dead. Bites covered his neck and fur, and paw marks were on the ground all around him, dozens of them.

We buried the grey invader and cried over him. The tom cats slid quietly back to their old ways. We

15

wouldn't hear of the grey cat again, we thought, we said.

But we were wrong, of course. Miss Telfer's stout tabby was the first, as, one by one, the mother cats produced their kittens; all grey. Grey after grey kitten was born in the village, some blue-grey, some dark grey, some pale grey, some with long fur, some with short. Patsy's was the last to be born. It, too, was grey, with white paws, white whiskers and a white tum. Patsy made a proud and perfect mother to the only kitten she ever had.

The invasion never came. I didn't think too much about it, anyway, apart from working out a few secret hiding-places. I was very busy with the important business of rearing kittens and looking after animals.

Only sometimes I'd wonder, and I still do, for this is a true story, just who was that cat, and where did he come from?

May Queen

told by Lizzie Barnes

Farmer Woolley's field, the twelve acre, has two ponds in it. One is a perfectly ordinary pond at the side of the road that runs past the field, with nothing remarkable about it except a large hawthorn bush on its bank with pink blossom instead of white, and an iron rail that we turned somersaults on—all of us except Dawn Taylor. She couldn't manage to get over, not that she was fat, but she had no spring in her, no spring at all, being heavy, big-boned and solid. This sounds awful, but really she was a very pretty girl with long dark-brown hair, blue eyes, a straight nose and a perfect Cupid's bow mouth.

"I have a perfect Cupid's bow mouth, my mother says," she would sometimes announce to us, as she stood looking in the cloakroom mirror at school. And since I have a great, big, gobby one, with the kind of teeth people call Tombstones, this did not greatly endear her to me. Nor did her being chosen as May Queen by our new Head-teacher, who was keen on bringing back the old festivals to our village. I didn't think much of this May Queen stuff, it sounded dead

17

boring to me, and what with specs and tombstones it didn't seem likely that I'd be chosen and I wasn't. But I didn't fancy being an attendant either, which is what I ended up as. Dawn is all right, really, with a nice nature, rather like a spaniel, and it's difficult to be horrible to her for long, though I did my best, being fed up at the thought of carrying her train and so on, for I did feel that being an attendant to anyone so stupid, however sweet-tempered, was a bit much. My partner in this train-bearing was a girl called Joan, bright and with-it, that one, but living outside the village in the new housing estate, so I did not play with her so often as Dawn.

Who, by now, had started to get really uppity, being an important figure at rehearsals, and what is worse, she had taken to reciting the items of her regalia, yes, she called it that, her crown, her sceptre, her orb, her velvet train, her long white gloves, her white satin dress, her seed-pearl necklace—what a load of boring rubbish, I said—but she took no notice as she continued with a long description of buying her white shoes and the man in the shop telling her mother that Dawn had the highest-arched foot he had ever seen. So have horses, I said, but she only looked at me as if I were some low, primeval form of life, and went on talking about her regalia. I shall go mad, I thought, as I rushed away and kicked a tree, which didn't hurt it at all, whereas I had to put a plaster on my blackened big toe.

I was to be dressed in yellow, a good colour on wasps, but hideous on me. My request to be allowed to keep my jeans on underneath the long frilled skirt was not considered, and Joan looked even worse in yellow than

I did, being freckled with more freckles than spaces if you see what I mean. She was totally uninterested in the whole project as she was sailing to Australia soon after, and did nothing but talk about Australia, so, what with Australia and regalia, I found the pair of them jolly boring, and escaped from them and the never-ending rehearsals as often as possible.

The evening before the great day found me in my favourite field, Farmer Woolley's, the twelve acre, you remember, that's a really big field, with Jeff Hobbs. I've never been Jeff's girl-friend, in fact Dawn was really, but I liked him much better than Steve Coates, who is supposed to be mine, I don't know why, as I haven't been able to stand the sight of him since we were both about five. Anyway, Jeff's a bit thick but nice. Boys do not have to be bright as long as they are good company and dishy. Well, that evening, Jeff and I made our way to the *other* pond in Woolley's field. Quite different, this one, from the road-side pond with the pink blossom and the iron rail that Dawn can't somersault over. This pond had atmosphere. This pond had mystery.

It was in the far corner of the field, and on the other side of it was a curving path, that rose quite high above it, and this path was so covered by bushes and plants and moss and shaded by tall, arching trees that, unless you knew, you would never have guessed that it was there at all. On the other side of this path was a smaller pond that shelved into a corn-field. Beside the ponds was a grove of beeches set in a strange circle that looked as if it meant something though I've no idea what, and I called the whole place Wonderland, which wasn't clever or original, but no one else thought up anything better. It was always dark in that corner of the field, the water had a blackish-green tinge beneath the trees, whose twisted and bulgy roots stretched deep into the pond, with moss growing up their trunks. Here even the flowers were different—not buttercups, daisies and dandelions like the rest (which was growing for hay) but Jack-by-the-Hedge and Lords and Ladies (you should have heard what Jeff called those) and a poisonous plant called Deadly Nightshade we weren't supposed to touch. But, best of all, over the further pond, which was supposed to be bottomless since it never dried up in summer like the other ones, there lay a round pole, like a telegraph pole, reaching from one side to the other, from the hidden path to the bank in the field.

We were going along to see if there were any interesting new developments in the way of nests or tadpoles, and we made our way very quietly and secretly round the edge of the field, almost under the hedge, because Farmer Woolley did not care for anyone in his field when it was growing for hay, so we were Indians pathfinding a new trail, and this took a long time, twelve acres being a fair-sized field as I said before, and when we arrived we climbed a tree to see if there were any Palefaces lurking.

One well-known Paleface was. Wobbling and stately, Dawn was slowly making her way round the outside. Instant boredom woke inside me.

"I thought she was having her hair done and then going to bed early," I sighed. However, as she approached we gave a wild Apache War Whoop and leapt off the branch together, just managing to miss her.

When she'd stopped screeching and got her breath back, we went on to the secret path, and sat on a mossy stump, looking at the pole lying so temptingly just above the green water. And, at that moment, two minds with but a single thought, Jeff and I decided that Dawn was going to walk across it. She hadn't said so, in fact she didn't know it as yet, but we knew. She had never yet dared to cross that pole. Tonight she would. Brave Dawn.

"I called for you," she told me reproachfully.

"You told me you were having a shampoo and blow-dry."

"I did. Don't you like it?"

"I liked it before. Straight."

"I needed waves and curls to keep the crown in place."

During this incredibly boring conversation Jeff got up and ran casually over the pole. There was no danger. He'd done it hundreds of times. The bottomless water gleamed green and cool.

"I'm wearing make-up tomorrow. Are you?"

"No."

"Well, I suppose it won't make much difference in your case. You could leave off your glasses, though."

I did not push her straight in. Instead I asked:

"How come you were let out?" Unlike Jeff and me, Dawn was an only, and the pride and joy of her mum and dad.

"I can only come for a moment. I felt all nervy, so my Mum said go and have a breath of fresh air, it will do you good, she said. I shall have to go back in a minute and check my regalia. The purple cloak, the white satin dress . . ." and she was off, reciting again.

Jeff crossed the log once more. I waited till he got to the other side, then I joined him, crossing over midway. We'd practised that one before, and it's fine as long as you don't look down. Seated on her mossy stump, Dawn had just reached the seed pearl necklace . . .

"What are you doing that for?" she burst out.

"For luck."

"What luck?"

"This pond is enchanted. That's why it's called Wonderland. And a dragon lives down in a secret cave in the water below, and on May Eve, that's now, you have to cross over the pole or he won't like it."

"What will he do?"

"He'll give you horrible bad luck."

"What sort of bad luck?"

"Oh, like breaking your ankle getting out of bed, if you're going to be a Queen in a procession or something like that. Or falling flat on your face with everybody laughing at you except your mother who's crying."

She was listening hard. At least, she'd stopped going through the regalia.

"I think I'd better go home now," she said, standing up.

"Just walk over the pole then, and it will all be all right."

"I don't want to."

"It's nothing," Jeff said. "Easy as falling off a log." I gave him a dirty look. Fine help he is. Dawn had got her mulish look.

"I don't believe in bad luck. My dad says it's all rubbish."

And suddenly, I was worried stiff, for this seemed to be a dangerous thing to say in Wonderland on May Eve. Was I imagining the trees stirring and clouds passing over the sun, a sudden chill in the air?

"You'd better walk over the log now, Dawn, or you may really get bad luck. I can just imagine the dragon, full of anger, down there."

I could too, by now, although I'd only just made him up.

Still she dithered.

"Come on, Dawnie," Jeff sang out from the other side. "I'll be here, to catch your hand."

He grinned. He has a nice grin, and Dawn took a cautious step towards him, and began to cross, too slowly, too nervously. Half-way across she wobbled and looked down at the still, mysterious, dragon-haunted, bottomless water. It was too much. She wobbled furiously.

"I'm coming," shouted Jeff.

"Don't look down!" I yelled.

She never did do what I told her. Jeff reached her too late, as astonishingly slowly, like a great pigeon, she leaned from one side to the other and fell . . . phlomph . . .

The water wasn't bottomless, of course, and somehow she heaved over to the bank, where we hauled her in, and there she was, safe, but squelching, wearing what looked like mud boots from the knees down. We were all plastered with mud, and Dawn's hair had lost most of its curl. We stared at each other. I waited for

Dawn to cry—she was bound to—I didn't blame her.

And she started to laugh. So did we. There on that bank, dripping with mud, we laughed and laughed and laughed.

"I'm sorry . . ." I spluttered, "about . . . hahahaha . . . your . . . hair . . . hahaha."

"I don't care." She was half-way between laughing and crying. "I was sick of May Queening, anyway, and everybody hating the sight of me and being horrible. Bother the regalia."

Jeff recovered first, struggling to his feet.

"Home," he said. He never talked much.

So we set off round the never-ending outside of the twelve-acre field, dragging a bit, especially Dawn on her mud feet. When we neared the last stile I said let's cut across the corner, and we were almost there, when a figure appeared, gaunt, menacing, stick in hand.

"Farmer Woolley! Run for it! Quick!"

We ran. Like murder, me in front. I flung myself over the stile just as Jeff and Dawn came up behind, Jeff tugging her along. Somehow, on the stile they collided, banged heads, and fell, a mixed-up heap. Jeff rolled neatly into the grass, but Dawn, as I told you, has no spring, no spring at all. Down she fell, like a cartload of bricks, splat . . .

The following day, the May Queen walked proudly but slowly and stiffly in front of her attendants. That was because her right knee and left ankle were heavily bandaged. Make-up hid the bruise on her forehead, though not the plaster on her nose. Her hair was straight and a bit tatty, but her cheeks were pink and she smiled beautifully at the photographers and admiring friends and relations from her perfect Cupid's bow mouth (undamaged). A great cheer went up for her.

Behind her followed a tall girl with freckles, and a small wicked-looking one with specs and big teeth. Mrs. Taylor has an enormous coloured photo of it all in the place of honour in their front room. We've only got a little one at home, but I don't mind.

Miss Piggy

told by Julie Bond

It must be wonderful to own an animal that you are proud of, a dog, say, that could frighten the fiercest burglar or even our Head-teacher, Mrs. Potts, just about the two most scary possibles I can think of. Imagine strolling gently through the park with a Great Dane or an Alsatian. If I had a dog like that I wouldn't have to hide behind the dusty old laurel bushes with my friends, Jason and Yasmine, when Merv Tucker and gang are looking for trouble and threatening to duff us up. He's known as the Iron Boy because he's so tough.

If I had a dog, a big dog, I think I'd call him Max.

"Show them, Max," I'd whisper to him, and Max would open his giant jaws, and snarl, and Merv Tucker and his gang would run away, squawking with terror, and I'd pretend to undo his lead, and they'd go even faster, home to their mothers.

Actually, I wouldn't dare undo a dog's lead in the park, as the park keeper is very hot on dogs being properly on their leads, and is always on the lookout for offenders, popping out from behind trees and under wheelbarrows when you least expect him, and I do not think he likes Yasmine and Jason and me much, after that time when Chilli—that's Jason's dog—got into the prize flower-bed. Chilli is a lovely dog, a tall, thin, sad red setter, and so gentle that if a burglar came through the window with a sack full of safe-breaking apparatus and two revolvers, she would wag her tail, lick him all over his face and pant WELCOME. It does seem to be our luck to have animals like that. Animals that are timid. Yasmine has twenty white mice, and they are extra timid even for white mice. I think this is sad, and that perhaps it's because our animals are like us, not very brave, not brave at all, really.

But even if that is so, I am not as awful as Miss Piggy. And I do hope that you are not taken in by this name.

No, it is not the famous and terrible television star that I am talking about. Miss Piggy is our cat, and my mother says no, I can't have another animal for a pet, not when I already have Miss Piggy. But I should very much like to have another animal, almost anything would do rather than that cat. My brother gave her that name. He's into punk and way-out humour, and he called her Miss Piggy for two reasons, he says—one, she's the ugliest cat he ever saw, and two, she's the stupidest . . .

My mother had called her Fluffy when she first came, but it was the name Miss Piggy that stuck.

She is a rare and unusual colour for a cat, dirty-yellow-grey, for she does not wash much, and round her neck is a khaki-coloured ruff. She has a tail like hairy string and a frilled car and green teeth.

"Don't let Miss Piggy bite you," my brother tells

28

people, "or you'll have to be jabbed against twenty different diseases, including bubonic plague."

But more than anything else, she is the most awful coward, even worse than the mice, or Chilli, or us. It doesn't seem possible that a member of the animal family that includes the tiger and the panther could be such a coward.

Not long ago, we had an outbreak of mice in the kitchen, which was because Yasmine had brought over some of hers one wet afternoon in the holidays, and they escaped and set up home together. A few days later my Mum spotted one of them doing a mad flit from the fridge to the sink, and she shrieked and carried on a bit, not that she's scared of mice, she says, but she doesn't like them about where there's food. My brother laughed.

"They're germ-free, compared with Miss Piggy," he said.

Still, my mother made me fetch Miss Piggy, who was fast asleep under my continental quilt, as she nearly always is. I think she's either naturally lazy or she feels safe there. She didn't like being disturbed and dragged the quilt on to the floor with her claws. In the kitchen she decided that grub-time must have arrived extra early, so she tottered over to the food bowl and sat beside it, looking hungry, with one paw outstretched.

"Get that mouse," ordered my mother. Miss Piggy looked back at her. It was obvious that the word "mouse" meant nothing to her, and, anyway, it had disappeared by now.

"Try catching your meals for a change," Mum went on, bitterly.

At that moment a twitching nose and long white whiskers appeared from behind an ironing-board in the corner.

"Get it," Mum yelled, hopping, and then, "Go on, chase them out of here!" for another one ran suddenly straight under the table and towards Miss Piggy. (Yasmine's mice are a bit stupid, I think.) The sight of a mouse rushing straight for her was just too much for Miss Piggy. With a yowl of terror, she leapt up on to a chair and stood there, trembling. My brother moved fast, grabbed both the mice in turn by their tails, swung them wickedly towards Miss Piggy, who nearly fell off the chair in fright, then popped them into a nearly empty cornflake packet and gave it to me.

"Your mate Yasmine might like these for her collection," he said, and winked.

"You ought to be ashamed of yourself, Miss Piggy," said Mum. "Fancy being afraid of two harmless little mice."

"What about you, Mum?" I thought, but didn't say.

The other day Miss Piggy did have an unusual fit of energy and chased a sparrow across the garden, which made a change as normally they chase her. The bird got away, of course, but in the meantime she had scrambled up a fruit-tree, a small apple-tree, so tiny that if I swing on the lowest branch my knees hit the ground. And there that cat sat, trembling, on this low branch, eyes screwed tight shut.

"There you are," I said to Yasmine and Jason. "You see. Not only is she afraid of mice, she's afraid of heights, as well."

"Vertigo," said Jason. He always knows words like that.

"I don't care what it's called, it's not right for a cat. Cats are supposed to be fearless hunters, leaping about on roofs and fighting. Put her on a roof and she'd drop off from sheer terror."

"Perhaps she's already lost eight of her nine lives and is taking good care of the last one," said Yasmine, lifting her down and making clucking noises, meant to comfort, I think, but sounding like a hen with hiccups. "Cowards can't help being cowards," she went on. She is a kind girl.

Those words came back to my mind when we took Chilli for her walk that evening, for who should appear but Merv, looking more like the Iron Boy than ever, with all his gang with him and a DOG. Paul Brickley, the gang's Number Two, was holding it with a chain as thick as its middle. This DOG had more teeth than I have ever seen on one animal other than a crocodile, and it was smiling generously with them. In size it was somewhere between a wolf and a pony. Merv prodded me in the chest, which I have never liked.

"Look at that, Jool. Just you take a look at that. That, you gotter admit, really looks like . . . a DAWG."

I admitted it. There wasn't much else I could do, as Paul Brickley was holding it so that it towered all over me, dribbling evilly. Merv prodded me again.

"Not much like that . . . thing . . , you've got there, is it?" He turned me with an Iron Hand so that I could see Chilli, who was sniffing a dandelion.

"Not much of a dawg, is it? You gotter admit it."

I admitted it again, as dreams of my huge Great

31

Dane or Alsatian called Max withered and died away for ever.

"And so," continued Merv, "you lot, keep out of our way, see? Or you and that grotty animal there will feel the weight of my fist."

He showed me the fist, clenched into bony lumps, then Paul showed me the dog's teeth, with saliva dribbling all over them. Then the gang went on its sunshiny way. We headed for home, not saying much. There didn't appear to be much to say.

"Cheeky lot," said Yasmine, at last, bravely. "I wanted to hit Merv."

I wanted to ask what had stopped her, but I didn't. I hadn't shown up very well either. 'Cowards can't help being cowards' kept going through my head, but it didn't comfort me much.

Spring came, at last. Blossom sprang out on the trees
and bushes, flowers bloomed, birds built nests, children
went tadpoling. My brother found three new girl-
friends. We discovered a place, a secret place, a hut in
the corner of the allotments (we never went to the park,
nowadays) and it was sheltered by a tall hedge, now
covered with fat, green, bursting buds. No one took
any notice of us or told us not to go there, so after a time
we did it up a bit, with mats and boxes. Chilli liked it,
flopping her long body over the floor like a red rug.
Yasmine brought one of her cages, and a couple of
mice, and then one evening Miss Piggy turned up,
purring like a rusty engine as she settled down.

"She won't hurt the mice, will she?" asked Yasmine.

"Don't be daft," I said, fiddling with the old tran-
sistor my brother had given me.

But one night we came to find the hut wrecked, comics torn up, the carpet thrown among the nettles, and food scattered. Yasmine had always taken the mice back home with her each night, which was a good thing, as the cage had been flung on the floor and the mouse-wheel wrecked. As we were trying to clean up the door was crashed open.

"Out, out, you lot!" shouted Merv. Paul, gang and the DOG were right behind him. "We're doing a takeover."

'Cowards can't help being cowards' ran through my brain again. Fat lot of good, that was. I wanted to push in Merv's beastly grinning face, to scream and shout and kick, but there were too many in the gang and they were bigger than us. It wasn't fair, it wasn't fair. We'd found the hut first, made it cosy, done it up. It was ours. Our place. And they were taking it, spoiling it, as they spoilt everything.

And like a hawk dropping from the sky on to a rabbit, down from the roof dropped Miss Piggy, right on to Merv's head, digging in her claws to hang on. Part of me thought, she's got it all wrong as usual, she thinks he's a rug or something like that. And he was yelling blue murder, so Miss Piggy dug in even deeper, as she hates loud noises, they make her nervous.

"Get it off! Get it off! Help!"

Paul's dog was snarling and tugging. Paul could hardly hold him. This frightened Miss Piggy even more, and she gave a terrible wail and launched herself on to its head, digging her claws right in. The dog howled a dreadful, dismal howl, and rushed off along the path, pulling Paul flat on his face and dragging him along over the rough ground. Then across the newly planted allotments rushed the dog madly, with Miss Piggy on his head, like a circus performer.

"Get those animals off the gardens!" went up the cry, and several gardeners joined in the chase. Paul had let go of the lead by now. Two of the gang went to him and two more tried to help Merv, who was feeling his head to see if it was still all there.

Yasmine, Jason and I, we looked at each other. Our time had come. The moment had arrived. We weren't cowards. No, not us.

We rushed at them, arms waving, feet kicking.

"Get out! Get out! It's our hut. Don't come here again!"

Even Chilli staggered to her feet and woofed at them, and then lay down again. How the gang ran. Like lightning.

They leave us alone these days. No one interferes with the hut. A rumour went around that Miss Piggy was gifted with magic powers, enabling her to get terrible revenge on anyone who offended her. I think my brother started it, at least he had a very funny look on his face when I told him this. Besides, though I don't think anyone else saw him, I know he was behind the hut with Anna Spence, his latest, that evening. Though he said, when I asked, that no, he didn't throw Miss Piggy over the roof on to Merv Tucker's head. But then you can never tell what he means or doesn't mean, 'cos of this way-out humour I told you about.

The funny thing is, though, that although I know Miss Piggy wasn't really being brave, she hasn't been so cowardly since. Yesterday she was chasing quite a large bird, a pigeon. Yasmine and Jason don't look quite so mouselike, either. And Chilli is going to have puppies. Me? Oh, well, I was never so much of a coward as the others, anyway.

Poor Arthur

told by Tom Kemp

After Dennis, the cat, had caught the white mouse one
day when the cage was being cleaned out—by Bloggs,
my stupid sister, of course—I wouldn't have let it
happen, only she's so slow, she didn't see Dennis
coming like a streak of death across the floor, up on to
the table, and to where that white mouse was just
running round and round, then Mum said there weren't
to be any more animals, because she couldn't stand
the smell, and she was the only one that fed them.

Well, we took to moaning about having no animals
except the cat, Dennis, you remember, and he's so old
I'm sure he was never a kitten, older than me and
always asleep except when he's hunting defenceless
birds and mice, and being all streaky and murderous,
and then we took to hanging around petshops and
looking at the creatures. I fancied a yellow spotted
snake and Bloggs a Great Dane, but we didn't have
much hopes of either, really, not with our mum.

Then, just at the right moment, our next door
neighbour said she'd got gerbils, and they were very

nice, and you didn't have to clean them out often as they didn't smell.

"All animals smell," said Mum.

The next door neighbour took us all round to the gerbillery, I suppose you could call it, as there were two couples and two sets of baby gerbils.

"I'll give you one for your birthday," she said, as I stood there letting them run over me, with my inside swimming with joy at the feel of their fur and their little soft claws. And Mum said all right, then, providing you look after them, not me.

So we cleaned up the old mouse cage, then rushed off to buy sawdust and gerbil food.

And so came Chuchi.

Not that we called her Chuchi at first. We tried Polly, and Nosey, and Cleo, but nothing fitted. She wasn't much to look at, a bit tatty, really, with ruffled fur and a big hooked nose which she poked into everything. But she had bright black eyes and she ran to us whenever we came near, head cocked on one side, chattering furiously, hiding nuts, eating nuts, tearing up toilet rolls, kicking angrily with her back feet when she was in a temper. Dad called her the little rat. He was always chatting to her or tempting her with peanuts so that she'd jump really high. Even Mum took to her. She let me have her in my bedroom because the cage didn't smell, and at night I'd let her run round my bed and snuggle in my pyjama pocket.

And she still hadn't got a name.

Only one day Mum said, out of the blue, "Let's go and get some grass seeds for Chuchi. She likes grass seeds."

"Chuchi?"

"Yes, Chuchi, of course," as if we ought to have

known all along. "That's the sound we make when we want her to come to us, and it's her funny chatter noise as well."

So there she was. Chuchi. Named at last.

Now all this time we'd kept an eye on Dennis, that hunting cat. There was no smell to tempt him, but he knew something very interesting was going on. Dennis is a clever cat. Watches and waits. Sometimes we'd find him outside my room, washing himself very innocently. Chuchi grew bad-tempered. Straw and shredded toilet rolls flew through the air.

"She needs a mate," Dad announced at tea-time.

"Babies," Bloggs cried, stupid eyes shining.

"I like Chuchi, but enough is enough," Mum said.

"Females need mating," Dad said. "That's why she's irritable. Females do get irritable."

"Humph," snorted Mum, banging down scrambled eggs on the table. I thought for a minute she was going to bang them on his head.

We bought another gerbil.

Dad built a second cage in case they didn't get on, and for the babies later.

This turned out to be a good thing, because Chuchi took a violent dislike to the new gerbil, and chased him out, biting and kicking like fury. He was terrified and squealed pitifully, poor little thing, only half her size. We called him Arthur. The next day we tried to put him in with her again, but it was no good. The cage was her territory and she wasn't having Arthur in it.

Then Dad thought of putting the cages together, and soon they were sniffing each other through the wire.

40

A week later they were both living happily in Chuchi's cage. Arthur grew bigger and braver but she was still the boss. They looked very alike now, though Chuchi still had the longer tail and the bigger nose, and a more untidy look.

Dennis the hunter waited, licking his tabby fur. Patient, wicked Dennis.

"I do wish she'd have babies," sighed Bloggs.

"Well, she's getting fatter," Mum said.

My dad drives a bus, and works different shifts. That day he'd gone to work very early, returned at ten in the morning, and gone out again at three. We came home with Mum, who's a teacher, at four. There was a note for us on the table. Dad in a temper is like Vesuvius erupting. The note said:

"If I find out who left the cage door open this morning, you'll wish you'd never been born, for that murdering cat has killed Chuchi. I've tried to catch him but he was too fast, which is just as well for him."

He'd put her on the sideboard, and she was stiff and cold, but her fur was as soft as ever. Mum was sobbing, and tears were streaming down Bloggs's face. I didn't cry. I just stood there, stroking her over and over again.

"We must bury her," Mum said, at last.

I found a Dinky car-container with a transparent top, and Bloggs put her inside, wrapped in cotton wool. Mum fetched some little flowers from the garden and put them in with her, and Bloggs drew a cross on a card and wrote, "Here lies Chuchi, the Beloved."

We dug a hole and placed her inside. The ground was hard. It hadn't rained for a long time.

41

Dad came home, face pale, anger gone.

"I loved the little rat," he said.

Mum stirred. "We ought to go and see if Arthur's all right. He must have been terrified when Dennis came out of nowhere and seized Chuchi."

We all trooped up to my bedroom, and Arthur was there, nervous and jittery; not surprising. Bloggs felt in the dark room Dad had built on above the cage, as a nursery, still crying.

"Now there'll never be any babies," and then:

"I can feel something. There's something here. The babies!"

"Let me see!" we all cried.

But we couldn't, for it had been made specially dark and quiet for the babies and the only way to see inside was to take the top off.

I fetched the screwdriver. Dad unscrewed the screws. Bloggs chewed her fingers. It seemed to take hours, but at last, there they lay, naked, pink, squirming, beautiful, four of them.

"But how can they survive," Mum whispered, "without Chuchi to feed them? I can't feed anything as small as that. They'll starve . . ."

Dad's face had turned even paler. Bloggs was crying again.

"No, I'll put them to sleep, first," he said.

At that moment Arthur jumped out of my hand, where I'd been stroking him for comfort, and ran across the room. We watched him. Perhaps Bloggs isn't so stupid as I've been saying all along, for she got it first.

"Look! Look! That's not Arthur! The tail's too long

and the nose is too big, and he's . . . she's heading for the babies! Dennis killed Arthur, not Chuchi! It's Chuchi! She's alive!"

Chuchi had reached the cage and the babies. She pulled them to her, and then all her blue and pink toilet paper, covered herself and the babies with it, and sat, glaring out of the heap, very angrily indeed, as if she didn't think much of us.

We were all grinning from ear to ear.

"Everything's going to be all right. The babies will live now."

"I'll put the roof back on so that they can be quiet," Dad said.

As he screwed in the screws, he started to laugh, a funny sort of laugh.

"What is it, Dad?"

"It's just that, well, poor old Arthur—he didn't have much of a life because Chuchi bullied him all the time, and when he dies he gets buried with someone else's name over him, and all of us smiling and happy because he's dead and not Chuchi. Poor old Arthur, I say."

"Poor Arthur," we all echoed, but we still didn't feel sad. Chuchi and the babies were going to live. Everything would be all right. Except for Arthur. Poor Arthur.

The Plagues

told by Simon Williams

The slightest bump in the road hurt. I groaned again and a sobbing howl of pain came from Bonkers, who lay between me and Petra on the back seat. She held his head on her lap and gazed out of the window, lost in some world of her own.

"We must be mad," said my father. The motorway sides swooshed past. "It's turning to snow."

Once Petra and I would have been excited by snow, but now . . . We drove on, even faster.

"How's the pain?" asked my mother, turning round from the front. I didn't bother to answer. Petra looked round from the window and said:

"It will be better soon."

"I still think this is madness," said my father irritably.

The windscreen wipers slid backwards, forwards, backwards, forwards.

"All we need to do is to get stuck on the motorway at this time of day in this weather, with Simon and the dog as ill as they are. I've a good mind to turn round at the next junction and go back home."

My dad's a big impatient man, plays rugger. I like football best, at least I used to, but I haven't played this term. He didn't want to be on this crazy expedition, didn't want to, at all.

Petra said, "Oh, Dad, we've been through it all, over and over again, and you promised to try it. Please."

"All right. All right. But I still think it's madness."

"Let's get off the motorway and have a snack or something," put in Mum.

"No," we all answered.

"Just get us there, and it'll be all right. You'll see."

Petra again. It seemed like she was the one in charge. The pain in my back which had lain quiet for a bit suddenly corkscrewed into me. I couldn't help moaning, and Bonkers whimpered. The pains always came for us both.

"Hurry," said my mother. "I can't stand much more of this."

Dad drove on faster into the almost deserted motorway, the snow falling finely like grains of salt.

It had been a smashing holiday. I hadn't fallen out with Dad much. We'd stayed in a caravan on the Lizard in Cornwall, the weather had been hot and every day we'd gone swimming and climbing, playing cricket on the beach. It seemed like centuries ago—that other Simon who threw down his bat and walked away because Petra got more runs than he did. But the best thing of the holiday was the puppy, Bonkers we called him 'cos he acted like he was crazy all the time, a fat, cream-coloured Labrador. I mustn't excite him

45

too much, Mum said, as he might have fits. It was great teasing him, though. He leapt in the curling waves after me, and slept on my bed at night, his fat tum all round and warm, and in the morning he would shove his way right down the bed and lick between my toes, which made me shriek with laughter and wake everyone up. Sometimes he tried to sleep on Petra's bed, but I didn't let him, he's mine, I said.

"He's mine, too," she flashed, then walked off. Later, "It doesn't matter," she said, and spent all day making a shell collection.

Holidays end, and we were in the car, heading for home.

"It's a long run, up north, son. Now, there's comics, butterscotch and apples. That should keep you occupied, so don't tease the dog, don't torment Petra, and don't kick the back of my seat. Got it clear?"

I don't like being told what to do or not to do, so I sat and sulked for a bit.

We were making a break on the journey at my Aunt Paula's house. She and Uncle Derek had just bought a guest house on the edge of Dartmoor. I liked her, she always made a fuss of me, but this year it was all—

"Isn't she pretty?" and

"I can't get over the way she's grown."

Nobody took any notice of me. I hadn't grown, apparently. Then Uncle Derek and Dad said they'd take us for a quick walk to stretch our legs before we got back in the car for the rest of the journey. We ran down their garden path, over the stile, set in a stone wall, into a field, and there it was.

A huge granite tor, dark grey, a melted helmet half

46

poured into the ground. I've seen and climbed tors before, but never one in an ordinary green field like this. It looked incredible, fantastic. From another side of the field a path ran to it. There was a notice at the bottom and an iron ladder up the side. We hurtled towards it. Petra got there first. ANCIENT MONUMENT the notice read, and then a lot more about not starting fires. The name struck me most.

"HELLTOR. What a smashing name. What a smashing place. Come on, let's go up."

"No," said Petra.

"You scared?"

"No. I just don't want to."

Dad and Uncle Derek caught us up, and Uncle Derek caught hold of her hand.

"Isn't it marvellous? Come on up with me. Don't be frightened."

"I'm not. At least, not like that." She seemed to be looking at Dad, at me, for some sort of answer, then shrugged and began to climb. I remember it all very clearly, perhaps because I suddenly felt very sick, too much clotted cream with that apple pie, I supposed, but I pushed them all out of the way and went to the front. I felt peculiar again climbing the iron ladder, sick and giddy and scared right through, but I've got used to that. Long ago, I found out I was afraid of heights and Petra wasn't. I never let on and I hid it by yelling and running and screaming.

"I wish you'd shut up for once," shouted Dad, coming up behind. The wind was strong and whistled all about us, as if it wanted to chip off hair or spare skin. We were all at the top, now. I hadn't watched

47

how Bonkers had got up that iron ladder, but now he was galloping round and round the tor at top speed.

"Look at that view," cried Uncle Derek, as if he'd made it himself.

We could see for miles, Dartmoor, lumpy and purple on one side and, on the other side of the tor, granite, dropping, down, down, down, like a cliff, to a patchwork of coloured fields and woods spreading to the horizon, far away against the blue sky. I loved that drop, and I hated it as well. Then I turned and started to chase Bonkers round and round, shouting a football chant, and throwing him down in a tackle, which he loved, going wild, barking and jumping about.

"Calm down," Dad yelled. "You'll fall off the edge."

I was always being told off. It wasn't fair. *She* wasn't being told off. *She* was standing there, hands in pockets, hair blowing, staring down the drop, staring, staring, absolutely still. Looked batty to me. But nobody told *her* off.

The tor was a saucer with a pool in the middle. Fed up, I crouched beside it, holding a wriggling Bonkers. The water was full of stones, many-coloured. Like a collection. I took one out. It was warm in my hand. I threw it into the pool, then fished it out again. It splashed, and Bonkers barked and barked like a mad dog, then made a puddle into the water. I rolled about, laughing my head off.

"Come on," shouted Dad. "I think I'd like to get back on the road. We've got a long drive in front of us. Let's hit the trail."

He picked up Bonkers and set off down the ladder. I pocketed the coloured stone and followed. Going

48

down was worse than going up had been. As we reached the bottom a long low roll of thunder sounded a long way away. Grey clouds were building up over the moor.

"Let's get a move on," called Dad, putting down the dog. "Now where's Petra got to?"

She was nowhere to be seen. I knew what he was going to say.

"Go back up and fetch her."

I thought of saying no, then thought again, having looked at Dad. I called to her from the bottom of the ladder but there was no answer. It looked menacing now, with dark shadows, spreading everywhere. I started to climb, hating it.

At the top of the tor, she was on her knees beside the pool.

"Oh, come on," I bawled, and shook her. She stared up at me as if she didn't know who I was, eyes clouded and dead as stones. So I shook her again. Bad enough having a mad dog without a mad sister as well. This time she stood up. By the time we were at the foot of the tor, the rain was lashing and spurting furiously, thunder and lightning overhead. But I'm not afraid of storms and I liked it, though we had to get dried off before we could start the journey.

On the way my head began to ache. So did my back. When we got home Mum took my temperature. It was 105, not that I cared. I roamed for mile after mile in a nightmare country where giant stones moved amid whirling duststorms, and serpents writhed in rocky pools. When I was better, Petra told me that Bonkers had been ill as well.

By this time, school had already started and I was keen to get back because I hoped to be in the football team that term. But the morning that I went back the school nurse inspected our heads, and I was sent home because I'd got more nits than she'd ever seen on one head, she told Mum, who was furious, and I had to stay at home until she'd cleared them. Mum didn't know where I'd got them from, for I hadn't been near anyone except my sister and she hadn't got any. Bonkers was covered with fleas, and not well, so he had to go to the vet.

Once more I returned to school, but on the first day I fell and broke my wrist. It didn't seem as if I would ever get to playing football. The same day Bonkers broke his front leg, a most unusual fracture said the vet, and he had to hop on three legs. At one time I would have fallen about laughing at this but something was changing my sense of humour. I read a lot and found the best time of the day was when Petra came home from school, because she played with me. I managed to get to school once more, and caught German measles, when no one else had it. Bonkers caught distemper which he'd already had his jabs against. After that, the nightmares came back as well. I caught mumps and sprained my ankle. But worst of all were the boils. I had boils all over me. Bonkers didn't like his much. The days blurred past, most of them spent in bed. Christmas was coming, not that I cared a lot. The other Simon, ages ago it seemed, used to make lists, long lists of all the things he wanted. This Simon didn't want much, only to go to school, and play football again, and not to feel ill all the time.

One day Mum remembered to fetch the holiday photos from the chemist. Together we looked at them. Could that fat, cream little dog be this sad animal with the scrawny coat? As for me, I was now taller than Petra, and as wide as a piece of string, a piece of string with boils on.

"Put them away," Mum sighed. "I can't bear to look at them."

Dad was working overtime, for vet's bills and medicine, he said, and then, I was only joking, Simon. He never told me off these days. As Mum put the photos away Petra ran out of the room and came back with my old anorak.

"I didn't think of it till I saw the photos. This is the one you wore that day, the last day before the holidays, before you were ill, and you haven't worn it since. . . ." She shook it and then felt in the pockets. "I'm sure there should be something here . . ." and she brought out the stone and held it in her hand, and her eyes were far-away and strange.

"Listen, Mum. Listen, Simon. We've got to take it back. Back to that tor. We've got to go back. And somebody's got to persuade Dad to take us."

"You can do that," said her mother. "He'll think we're mad."

We were off the motorway now, the snowflakes fatter, thicker.

"They know we're coming?" asked Dad. He sounded tired.

"Yes, they'll be ready for us."

They were: Uncle Derek and Aunt Paula outside

with torches. She and Mum kissed one another. Snow swirled all around us.

"It's like something out of Dickens," Dad muttered as he got me on his back. It hurt. "Sorry for all this, Derek, Paula. Dragging you out like this. You must think we've gone crazy. Oh, damn this snow. Look, I don't know what to say."

"Don't say it then. Just you do what you think you have to, and we'll help if we can."

Petra led the way with a torch. All around, as the snow fell, the air bubbled and seethed. We plodded our way in endless silence, Dad holding me. The wind banged and hit us as we climbed the lower slopes of the tor.

Somewhere a dog howled, and it wasn't Bonkers. The air was full of other things as well as snow. Once, my father slipped and swore. I could see the light of Petra's torch as she climbed the ladder. Mum fell and cried out.

"Keep going," called out Petra.

At the steps I pushed down off Dad's back. I knew I could.

"On my own. Please."

It was the worst bit, the fear bit. But it was dark and I wasn't afraid of being afraid any more. There are worse things.

We reached the top and Bonkers was beside me, nose thrust into my hand. I knelt beside the saucer pool, one arm round him, the other feeling in my pocket for the stone, while the wind blew straight from my nightmare land, trying to fling us off the tor. I placed the stone in the pool. I had to break the ice.

"Sorry," I muttered. "And Bonkers is." He licked my face and I ached with loving him. But the other ache, the pain, had gone. *I didn't hurt at all*. Petra's torch shone bright. Bonkers shook the snow off him and frisked his legs. His tail was wagging. I felt very strange, not knowing what to do.

"Is that all?" I asked my sister.

She shone her torch round the top of the tor, past the group of grown-ups standing, lost, together.

"We can go now," she said, then awkwardly dropped on her knees beside the icy pool. The others moved towards the ladder.

"Whatever is it all about?" hissed Aunt Paula.

I stretched out my arms. I didn't hurt at all, anywhere.

"Are you all right, lad?" called Uncle Derek.

"Come along, Petra, must you kneel there, like that? You'll catch your death," called out my mother.

"Yes, come on, I need a drink." My father's voice was irritable. He'd had enough. "I hope we're allowed to go now, Petra, if it's all over. She's running this show, you know, Derek. She's in charge. Madness to me. And if what she says is right, I reckon it was a pretty severe punishment for a very little sin. Are you all tight now, lad? Though I can't say I really believe in all this rubbish . . ."

Petra's voice rang through the air, the wind, the snow.

"Stop it! Stop! Oh, can't you see? Don't you understand? Even now?"

"Sorry, sorry," my father muttered, and we hurried down the ladder towards the light and warmth that awaited us. The snow had stopped before we reached the house.

(With apologies to that most frightening of tors.)

Toothie and Cat

High on the hills above the city was a cave, well hidden away among the trees and the rocks and the bracken. And in that cave lived an old tramp with a gingery, greyish beard hanging to his waist, a greasy hat on his head, string tied just below the knees of his trousers, and one tooth that stuck out over his beard. Because of this he was known as Toothie, and he couldn't remember any other name. He couldn't remember very much at all, for his brain was as foggy as a November night. He was never bright even in his prime and he hadn't improved with the years. Nobody had ever cared for him much ever since his mother dumped him, wrapped in an old blanket, outside a police station, and then made off as fast as she could. Toothie tried to keep away from police stations ever after.

Below the hills in the city lived Cat, Cat the Black and the Bad, a streak of a cat with claws as sharp as daggers and a heart as black as his tatty fur. No one loved Cat. Once he was dropped in a river and left to drown. But you don't drown animals like Cat that easily. He got out, and survived, by hatred, mostly.

He hated people and children and bright lights and kindness. He loved fighting and stealing, roof-tops and alleys and, most of all, dustbins. He relied on them when the birds grew careful, or too many kitchen doors were shut. In the day-time he thieved and slept on walls in patches of sunlight. At night he rampaged across roof-tops, wailing and caterwauling. So he lived for some years, till one morning he dropped from a roof-top a bit carelessly, and a car speeding through the dawn grazed his leg. Snarling and swearing, he limped to the side of the road, where Toothie, who had also been raiding dustbins, found him. He was pleased, for he'd found a very meaty chicken carcase.

He walked all round Cat, who spat at him. Then he popped a bit of chicken into the complaining mouth, and Cat stopped spitting, and ate instead. Toothie popped him in his old bag, and went back to the cave,

where he made some chicken soup and tied a big leaf round the injured leg. After a time Cat stopped spitting at him, for he'd grown to like Toothie's smell. His leg healed.

Cat did not return to the city. It was summer. He hunted and Toothie cooked: stews and soups in his iron pot, other tasty dishes baked in mud packed at the base of the fire. Long warm days passed by in the green wood and the dark cave. Sometimes Toothie would sing and Cat purr, both rusty noises. That autumn was beautiful, warm and golden, with more nuts than had been seen for years. Toothie and Cat were well fed and content.

Until the night the October wind arrived, blowing cold, stripping the leaves off the trees, and it brought with it the sound of cats singing in the city below. Cat stirred in his sleep and woke up. He left Toothie's warmth to sit in the mouth of the cave, listening. Yes, there, again, came the yowling of cats. Cat shivered. He looked once at the old man, asleep, and slipped out into the night.

A fortnight later he came back, hungry, limping, wet and exhausted, longing for Toothie's warm fire, Toothie's food, Toothie's smelly company. But the cave was empty. The iron pot hung forlornly by the burnt-out fire. Toothie had gone.

Cat sat and washed himself, which is what cats do when they don't know what to do next. Then he searched through the woods, crying his strange, wild call. There was no Toothie. Cat slew an unwary bird who would have done better to have migrated and, still hungry, set off for the city.

58

Through the streets he ran, sniffing, investigating, fighting, always searching for Toothie's fascinating smell, and one day, a week or so later, he arrived at the City Hospital and knew that his friend was inside.

Now Cat was much cleverer than Toothie, and he knew from the smell of the hospital that that was where people were ill, and his cat brain put illness and chicken together. He'd got to find some chicken.

He tried as many houses as he had paws before he finally crept into a gleaming, shiny bright kitchen, and there on the immaculate tiled surface lay a scrumptious chicken leg on a plate of crisp salad. The salad Cat ignored, he was not a lettuce-eater, but he seized the chicken and was just about to leap through the partially opened window when the owner appeared, screamed like a whistling kettle and spent the rest of the day feeling very ill indeed, and telling anyone who could be made to listen how a fiendish monster had appeared like a black demon in her sacred kitchen. Cat kept increasing in size till he reached the dimensions of a mini-tiger.

A while later, the mini-tiger sat outside the hospital door and waited, chicken portion gripped firmly in teeth. Going in at the front door didn't seem like a good idea—it looked too busy and important. Cat had never liked front doors, anyway. Back or side doors were for the likes of him. So he slunk round the corner till he came to a dark staircase that went up and up and on and on. Right at the top were dozens of dustbins. Cat purred through the chicken. He liked those dustbins, homely and friendly, they were.

Beyond them was a door with two little round glass

panels. It opened in the middle and swung as someone walked through. And Cat slid in, keeping a very low profile. He ran, chicken in mouth and stomach almost on the floor, through rows of beds, and then into another ward with yet more beds. In the third a little boy lay in bed, bored. He sat up and cried:

"There's cat. It's got something in its mouth. Good ole puss cat. Come here."

He wanted Cat a lot, but Cat ran on. But now that he was spotted, pandemonium broke loose.

"Catch that cat!"

"Stop him!"

"Get that filthy animal out of here!"

As fast as he could, Cat ran on. Patients shouted as nurses ran to grab him.

But nothing could stop Cat now. Like a rocket swooshing into space, Cat shot down the ward to find Toothie. He dodged trolleys, ran under beds, ran over beds, squeezed between legs, narrowly missed cleaners, tripped up nurses carrying vases of flowers or trays, scattering people right and left to reach the bed with the screens round it where Toothie lay dying.

He'd collapsed with pneumonia a week after Cat had left him and somehow, shivering, coughing, full of pains, he'd crawled to the road, where a bus driver had driven him straight to the hospital despite complaints from some of the passengers. And since then, Toothie had lain in terror of the bright lights, the uniforms, the smells and the sounds, all too much for his mazed mind. He wanted to die.

Sister's voice rang out loud and clear.

"Stop that beast! It's got germs!"

60

Hands grabbed at Cat, missing narrowly. He shot through the screens and the doctor and nurses beside Toothie and up on to the bed. There on the whiter than white, brighter than bright, snowy, frosty, bleached, purified, disinfected, sterilised, decontaminated pillow Cat laid the dusty, greasy, tooth-marked chicken leg, just beside Toothie's head.

Shouts were all about him now.

But Toothie's eyes opened and he saw Cat. A triumphant burst of purring sounded through the ward. Come what might, Cat had arrived. He'd found Toothie.

The Long Crawl

told by Lizzie Barnes

I twisted my ankle the evening before Sports Day, and I was hopping mad about it, which is the only way you can be about a twisted ankle, being both painful and unwanted, like a rotten tooth. Furthermore it was not my fault at all, I was just minding my own business, coming out of the fish and chippery or the Chinky, depending on what you fancy at the time, cod'n'chips or sweet and sour (I'd got beefburgers), when Spider Hobbs, the mad brother of a friend of mine, tripped me up in the doorway, so that I fell flat on my face in the beefburgers, which, in a way, was a good thing as my specs didn't break, but got instant grease instead, so that I couldn't see, and I did not find it at all funny, especially as the five thousand spectators did, and were roaring their heads off, just like the Romans laughing at the poor, suffering Christians in the Colosseum, and when I got around to standing up there was this agony in my right foot, and I could hardly walk. My friend, Jeff Hobbs, helped me home, not far away, while I could hear Spider laughing fit to burst behind me, and I thought, right, I'll get you later, but, mainly, at the time, I was worrying about not being in the Sports next day.

This worry proved only too correct. Despite Dad's efforts with cold compresses, witch hazel, and bandages, my foot swelled up and up to the size of a purple melon, and the person who was not going to win the high jump and the hundred metres was me. And believe me, before Spider and Fate tripped me up I stood a good chance. I won both last year, just beating Linda Holmes into second place, and though Patti Jones had arrived since then, I thought I could still win, despite her being nine metres high with legs to match and coming from the West Indies and a family of super athletes. I tried to keep the bedclothes off my aching foot and cried.

We compete for houses, not ourselves, my house being Vikings—we won the Trophy last year, the others being Romans, Saxons, and Normans, boo, I can't stand the Normans, wish they'd never invaded us. From this you can see that our Head-teacher is a History fiend. There is a fair amount of rivalry about who is to get the Trophy this year.

Despite bandages from knee to toe, I was determined to go to school so as not to miss anything, and so Dad drove me to school, a rare treat, and delivered me up to our class teacher, Mr. Higgins, who is a very nice man, and came with the school, I think, they have the same well-worn look. Dawn, my beautiful but dim friend, once asked him if it was frightening living at the time of the Black Death, and he said no, it wasn't as bad as living in a cave with the sabre-toothed tigers roaming about, so there is not much wrong with his humour, though Dawn believed every word and gave him the hideous knitted egg cosy she'd made, to make his life a bit comfier she said. Since egg cosies are one of the most useless things on the face of the earth, it didn't seem likely, but he thanked her kindly, and said it would make a big difference next time he was living in a cave.

Anyway, he was kind to me, too, when I croffled in, feeling about ninety-eight at the last birthday, and said that I could help him score so that I should not feel out of things, in fact, they were all kind to me, except Spider Hobbs and I did not speak to him. But I still felt mean and envious when I saw Linda and Patti in their kit, limbering up. Amongst the rest, this year there was to be a new athletics event, throwing the discus, and both of them were determined to win it.

I could tell you who was not going to win anything, who hates all Games and Sport, and who nearly drove me out of my mind that morning with moaning on and on, and that was my friend, Dawn.

"I didn't sleep last night," she began, during Maths.

"Neither did I," I replied, struggling with a work card on percentages, horrible things.

"It was my nerves," she went on.

"It was my foot."

"Oh, but you haven't got anything at all to worry about, since you've managed to get out of everything."

"But I didn't want to get out of anything."

"I think you're lucky."

"I don't."

"I can't bear to think of it. All those people watching."

"Don't worry. You can only come last."

"I don't want to disappoint my mother."

"Since you've come last in every race you've been in since you came to this school ages ago, she isn't likely to be disappointed this year. She must have got used to it."

"I don't think that's very nice, Lizzie Barnes. I might win something."

"Dawn, pigs might fly, and I might get this sum right, and you might win a race, but none of 'em are likely."

She turned her big blue eyes on me, hurt at such cruelty, but Mr. Higgins suggested that it might be a good idea to do a little work for a change, and I was relieved to be quiet and ache and be miserable in peace. At play-time everyone jabbered away like mad about the Sports and I felt left out. My foot throbbed, so I grabbed a paperback on Heroes of the Past Who Achieved Great Things, and sat not reading, for my eyes seemed all gummed up although I wasn't crying. Patti came across and said in her soft voice, "It's not the same without you to run against," and I was just going to tell her how fed up I was, when Dawn joined us to say how scared she was of the obstacle race she was in, and that, at the last moment, to replace me, she'd been put down for throwing the discus. Some of us had had some practice in this, but Dawn hardly knew what a discus was, let alone what to do with it.

In the afternoon we set off for the big sports field, about half a mile away, that is, the whole school set off in a long trail like a furry caterpillar in its green and

65

yellow kit, and I drove away in a car with the Head-teacher who was driving there to see that everything was ready in advance. I felt peculiar and grand driving past them all, and Spider Hobbs put out his tongue, so I just stuck my nose in the air. At the field the Head-teacher told me to hop up to the table where Mr. Higgins was to be scoring, so I crawled up to the stand and sat down awkwardly at the edge of a chair, feeling like a twit, but the school eventually churned into the field and each class sat down in its place with its teachers and helpers. The air buzzed with anticipation. Parents were arriving with small brothers and sisters. Not mine. Mine were at work, and my kid brother and sister were in the first school, which hadn't come to this Sports—they have one of their own.

Sitting where I was between Mr. Higgins and the Head-teacher with the school loud-hailer, I had a good view of everything, Linda and Patti, and Dawn, pale with terror. And it seemed silly that she should be out there, having to do something she didn't want to do, while I was perched up on a stand, not doing what I wanted to.

Each house had its colour, Romans blue, Saxons yellow, Vikings red, hoo-ray, and Normans green, boo. Cards had been made out with 1, 2 or 3 on them, and these were handed to the winners as they arrived at the tape. The winners brought them to me and I read them to Mr. Higgins, who totted up the score and wrote it on the score board.

The afternoon's events began, as they always did, with the Head-teacher speaking gibberish through the loud-hailer—it never works properly—first and second

66

year before the interval, third and fourth after. I felt
mixed up about the result. Of course I wanted my
house to win but I didn't want it to do too well without
me competing, so I finally decided that I'd like them
to win by one point with someone saying to me, of
course Vikings would have done better with you taking
part. That settled, everything started to happen
quickly and I didn't have time to feel sorry for myself.
The sun shone, but it wasn't too hot, and at half-time I
was given a cup of tea with the staff and parents, which
was super, except I did think as I nibbled one of Mr.
Higgins's biscuits that the ones who needed the refresh-
ment most, the children, weren't getting any. By now,
I felt like part of the Staff and took no notice when
Spider Hobbs made an excuse to come up to the stand
and whisper Creepy Crawly, Lizzie Pawley in my ear
as it was so babyish.

By half-time the score was this: Romans 78, Saxons
75, Vikings 70 and Normans 61.

After the break, the Sports started up again, and now
it grew more interesting as my friends were competing.
When it was the fourth year's turn, Patti won the hundred metres, Linda the high jump, Patti the long jump,
Jeff the boys' hundred metres, Spider the boys' hurd-
ling—I hoped he'd catch his foot and fall over, but he
didn't. And it was discus time. A dreadful, awful,
ghastly and horrible boy called Walter J. Crow won
the boys' event; then six girls took up positions, three
in front, and the other three about six yards behind,
Dawn in the front row, which didn't seem a good idea
to me. She was wobbling like a blancmange, the rather
slow and stately wobble she does when she is nervous,

because it was her first event. Mr. Higgins doesn't put her in track events any more, because she cannot keep in a lane and two years ago shot straight across the field, causing a pile-up, and Angie Bates had to be taken to the Out-patients. Remembering this, I wondered if Mr. Higgins should have put her in the obstacle race, but he doesn't like leaving anybody out, just have a go and it doesn't matter he says.

Throwing a discus is a bit like hurling a flying saucer, the size of a plate but thicker. Dawn gripped hers, spun round and round, hurled it, and plonk, Linda Holmes is lying flat on the ground. Dawn's discus had gone backwards instead of forwards. Proceedings were halted while Linda was revived and Dawn calmed,

and the agitated parents settled once more. Finally, things began again, egg-and-spoon, sack, three-legged, won by Jeff and Spider, and the relay. Only the two obstacle races remained—they're always last because of the clearing away—and the score was now Romans 156 points, Vikings 154 points, Saxons 148 points, and Normans 139, hooray, they're last.

The obstacles were assembled and I was sorry I wasn't doing it instead of Dawn, who came up to the stand to ask if she could be let off, but Mr. Higgins said she was the only girl Viking left available, so she went away agreeing—to her execution, from the sad look of her walking back to her place.

The course was hard. Balancing along an upturned

form, handspring on a mat, ten-yard stretch with a skipping-rope, vault over the horse, jump through a hoop, leap over the box, throw three balls into a basket, pick out the last and crawl with it under a big black plastic tarpaulin, and run to the finishing-line.

Walter J. Crow won the boys' obstacle, yuck, then the girls lined up.

Dawn started off quite well, balancing on the form, despite wobbles. Handsprings were impossible but she rolled, getting a bit tangled up with her long hair, but struggling on with the skipping. Vaults had always proved a mystery to Dawn, but she hauled herself over gamely, though she was now in her usual place of last. And I found I was sitting there saying, Come on, old girl, you can do it, come on, Dawn, and willing her with every bit of my useless power just to get to the other end, because she was trying so hard when she didn't want to. Somehow she arrived at the tarpaulin, held down at the sides by lots of second-year feet. But as she struggled under, Angie Bates emerged at the other end and ran to the tape, and a great roar went up, for Angie and for Vikings, now ahead. One by one, the girls came out from under the plastic and Vikings had won by one point, and the crowd went mad, children starting to run all over the field and up to their parents. The second years holding down the tarpaulin were stamping up and down and yelling.

But I didn't care if we'd won, for Dawn was still under the tarpaulin. I'd watched and watched and knew she hadn't appeared.

She'd be trampled to death!

I shouted to Mr. Higgins but he didn't hear.

70

I shouted even louder, but the noise was deafening. I wished I could get to her. Curses on my ankle.

"Hello, horrible," bellowed a voice.

"Spider," I shrieked, "Dawn's still under there!"

"Right," he yelled back, and I forgave him my ankle—the lot—as he pushed through the crowd to find her.

On the table lay Mr. Higgins's whistle. I picked it up and shoved it at him. He must have seen the look on my face, for he blew it, loud and long.

And silence fell.

And in the silence, her face mudstained, hair tangled, eyes enormous against the light, Dawn crawled out into the daylight, at the wrong end, the starting end, having turned completely round as she went. Spider, arriving panting beside her, yelled at the top of his voice:

"Three cheers for Dawn, the best loser of the lot!"

And a mighty cheer went up, as Dawn, just not crying, but only just, gave her beautiful smile and looked round to see if her mother was watching.

Joe's Cat

The cow parsley stood higher than his head as Joe
Sprague whistled his way along the lane that led home.
He carried a large bag with his cricket gear in it and
he whistled because he'd just made sixty-nine runs for
his team, the highest score in the last match of the year.
Joe loved cricket. His dad played in the village cricket
team, and Joe scored for them, and he would play for
the team when he grew up. Only one thing he liked
better than cricket and that was football, and soon the
season would be starting and Joe in his second year at
the County Comprehensive would have a good chance
of playing for the second team. The school had a fine
Games record and the first team were the County
Champions, but Joe felt fairly sure of a place because
he knew he was good. But before then, the summer
holidays were nearly here, long days of helping Dad on
the farm, and camping with his mates in the last week
of August. And so, Joe whistled even louder as he made
his way along the lane to the thatched cottage where he
lived, a cottage so beautiful he did not even notice that
it was.

He noticed the kitten, though.

It lay in the tufty, seeding grass that grew down the middle of the lane, where too few cars ever travelled to keep the grass down. The kitten lay so still that when Joe bent down and touched it he thought it was dead. But the thin chest moved up and down like a whisper. Joe stroked the little body very gently and the kitten stirred and rasped his hand feebly with a rough tongue. He picked it up, cradled it in one arm—it weighed as much as a leaf—picked up his bag and went on his way. He was ravenously hungry by now, and had no doubt that his mother would feed the animal, as she did everything and everybody finding their way to the door.

The ham and eggs and chips and fruit pie and cream were delicious, in fact all his meals were so good that he took them for granted. He gave the kitten some milk and it slept in a corner. The other animals took no notice of it, there were so many in Joe's house that they didn't get jealous of one another but lived together with a fair amount of toleration. There was nothing wrong with the kitten, only it was very weak, as if it might have been shut away in the dark for a while with no food. No one objected to its being around. Sometimes children at school would say that they weren't allowed to have a cat or a dog or a hamster or whatever it was they fancied. Joe did not even try to understand this. A world without animals he could not imagine, it would be like a world without seasons or football and cricket.

The kitten grew fatter and stronger, and very playful. It especially liked the rabbit's foot tied to a piece of string that Joe would trail along the floor for it to pounce on, pretending it was a rat. And as it grew stronger, it grew bolder, disappearing for large parts of the day into the farmyard, but always returning for its food. It was a tom kitten, and Joe called it Boots, on account of its wide furry legs. None of the other animals bothered it much. School broke up, the holidays began and Joe at last went camping.

It was a wonderful holiday, marvellous weather, everything perfect. Only, the day Joe came home his father was killed by a tractor overturning on him at Wither's Edge, a steep field with a wooded stream in it where Joe and his mother used to picnic when he was a little boy.

There were two Joes, he sometimes thought, the Joe that had been, and now, this one who stood outside himself and watched and helped, as his mother, doing everything as carefully as ever, packed the furniture and all their things, and arranged for their successors at the cottage to have the animals, as there were none allowed in the city flat, where they were going to live to be near his mother's work. Apparently the cottage did not belong to them but had only been rented while their father had the job that went with it, and they did not have enough money to buy a house, and there were no jobs for his mother in the country. She had worked in a clothing factory before she married Joe's father, and at this she could earn enough to keep them now. She had loved the farm, running the garden and the dairy, but those days were gone.

She did not cry. Neither did Joe, and it would have

been better if they had. But they were quiet people, Joe and his mother.

And it was even quieter in the flat alone all day, knowing no one, his mother out at work. Joe had never been lonely before, had not known what loneliness was. But now he knew. His mother came home almost too tired to talk. They ate their meal, silently, and went to bed.

So he was glad when school started.

Only, it was terrible.

Joe had not realised he was so slow. He'd gone, at five, to the village school, where he managed his reading and maths, and then to the County Comprehensive, where his skill at games had made him well liked and by hard work he had kept up, but here, here it was different. In a vast, dirty building surrounded by asphalt and railings, called the annexe—you went to a huge, new complex in the third and fourth year—Joe was hopelessly lost. The plan and timetable of the school were so complicated that Joe never had any idea where he was supposed to be and why. No one explained anything, and he was too shy to ask. Somehow, he just got brushed aside and submerged in enormous queues, it seemed they queued for everything. Meals, for instance; there was a choice of menu, but that choice had always gone by the time Joe arrived at the front. He couldn't quite keep up, with his work, with anything, he was always not quite ready, not quite there, he couldn't get to sleep at night and when he did, the nightmares were horrifying. He grew tall and thin instead of short and stocky. His summer tan faded.

Football. He pinned his hopes on football. He had to make a break-through with that, for it would bring fun, and with it, friendship.

The first practice was with a master with eyes and a tongue as sharp as needles. Joe didn't especially shine but he didn't make a fool of himself either. He made some useful passes, scored a goal, and found his name up on the board for another practice next day.

And he messed up the entire game. He had never played so badly in the whole of his life. Late that night, unable to sleep for thinking of it, he got up, at last, to get a drink, and as he moved about in the cramped flat, he remembered how sometimes in summer he would get up and wander about, and smell the honeysuckle and the roses, instead of the diesel fumes from the lorries roaring past, and the animals would stir and greet him lazily, rubbing round his legs.

He heard a noise. It was his mother crying for the first time. He went into her room, sat on the bed, put his arms round her and they cried together.

It was late when he awoke, for he had forgotten his alarm, and his mother had already gone to work. In the tiny kitchen with just a sink and a kitchen cabinet, so different from the kitchen at the cottage, he helped himself to cornflakes, carried them back to the livingroom and bent to light the gas fire. There in front of it, fast asleep, was Boots.

Boots woke up, wrapped himself round Joe's legs, and purred with a full-blooded roar. In fact, he had grown into a pretty full-blooded cat by now, heavy and powerful, with big, furry legs. He stretched his long length up to the table, cheekily stuck his paw into the bowl of cornflakes and scooped some out. Joe didn't mind, for he had little appetite these days, so he put them on the floor, where they rapidly disappeared into Boots's tum. Then he leapt on to Joe's lap and listened attentively while Joe talked about everything, how lonely he was, how he missed his dad, how he hated seeing his mum so miserable, how he was useless at school, how he couldn't play football any more, and how he hated the city. Boots twitched an ear, and licked Joe's hand with his harsh tongue. It was fairly obvious that Joe was not going to get to school that day, so after a while, Joe got dressed, raided the reserve tin money, and travelled back to his old home on the bus, accompanied by the cat.

"I'd like to keep you," he said to it. "But there's just no way."

It felt strange walking up the lane with the grass growing down the middle, unreal somehow, perhaps because he'd grown so much that everything looked smaller. A youngish woman answered the door.

"What do you want?"

"I used to live here. I—I brought back the cat."

"What cat?"

Boots had run off as soon as Joe put him down, off to investigate the farmyard, as usual.

The woman looked harassed. A few spots of rain fell.

"Come in for a minute, if you like."

The house looked sharp and ugly to Joe. It wasn't the same place. He asked about the animals, for there were none in the kitchen.

"They're outside. I don't like them indoors. I couldn't keep track of them all."

Upstairs a baby started to cry.

"I'll have to go, I'm sorry," she said. "Can I get you a cup of tea or something?"

The baby wailed even louder.

"No, thanks. I'd better go."

A flurry of wind followed him down the lane. He looked back once or twice but could see no sign of the cat, ungrateful animal, he thought. Nearly back at home he passed a florist's and, feeling daft but determined, he bought a bunch of flowers for his mother. Once in the flat, he put them in water and began to prepare a meal.

Boots was asleep in front of the gas fire.

This time, Joe made no attempt to guess how the cat had got in. He was just there, that was all, and he wasn't taking him back again at this time of day, no thanks.

"My, that smells good," said his mother, coming in, "and those flowers, where did they come from? They're lovely."

"Look who's here . . ." he began, but the doorbell rang; their landlady, who seemed to have taken to them.

"Now, I can't stop . . ." she was a woman who hurried all the time . . . "downstairs tenant . . . leaving . . . flat vacant . . . from next week . . . garden . . . you'd like that . . . only a pound a week extra . . . paper round for the lad . . . know somebody . . . I'll fix it . . ."

And she was gone. Later, his mother said:

"I'll rent a TV set and make some new curtains.

And if we have a garden I can plant some bulbs for the spring, and maybe we'll have an animal again, a cat perhaps?"

Boots purred with great vibration from his seat on Joe's knee.

"We can keep him then?" he asked, but his mother was reading the paper and didn't answer.

But next day, Joe had the old sick feeling again. School. School. Failure. Misery.

The first lesson was Language, which Joe used to call English in his old school. It might have a different name but what they had to do seemed familiar, write a description of a scene you know well. Joe had never been able to write descriptions, except for one he'd done of a tractor years ago, and he didn't exactly fancy that now. His hands turned to feet somehow when it came to writing, and those feet had none of the wizardry that they could sometimes—though not lately—show on the field.

But as he sat there something wrapped round his legs under the table. He shot down a hand, a furry face rubbed against it and a harsh tongue licked it. Good Lord, Boots was here. That cat had a genius for getting into places. Well, they'd better both keep quiet, or there would be trouble. He looked round furtively. No one appeared to have noticed anything. Best thing was to start writing and pray that Boots sat quietly till mid-morning. Joe picked up his pen, and the sights and smells and sounds of the farmyard came to him so vividly that the words flowed out of his head and poured down the page. He had never in his life written like that. The buzzer, usually so long and anxiously awaited, rang before he'd finished.

"Can I go on with it later?" he asked the teacher. He noticed in surprise that she had a kind and pleasant face.

"Miss Downes," she prompted, smiling. "Of course you can. And oh, Joe, do come and see me if you are worried about anything."

He'd got outside before he remembered Boots, but when he returned to the classroom there was no sign of the cat anywhere. A West Indian girl stood by the door, very pretty, and laughing. She terrified him, he was always shy of girls, and the girls in this class seemed so sharp and clever and shiny, somehow. Then she stopped laughing and smiled at him, instead.

"Come with us, and we'll show you around. Reckon you might need a bit of looking after."

Suddenly he was surrounded by three of them and scared out of his wits, but then a boy appeared out of nowhere, a boy he'd noticed before and liked, a boy who was very nippy with a football.

Together they all made their way into the playground.

Joe found his name on the practice list again. And this time he was determined to do well. He had friends now, lots of them, but especially Mark, the footballer, and Davina, the girl who had spoken to him first. He felt happy and confident as he ran on to the pitch.

Yet some of his old skill had left him, try as he might, and after ten minutes or so, a wave of such misery swept over him that he felt like running off the pitch and leaving everything. And out of the blue, through the tears that blurred his sight, a furry figure appeared, standing on bulky back legs, and, trapping the ball in them, he sent it direct to Joe, who scored a superb goal. Next day his name went up among the team.

He walked home with Mark and Davina. When he got in Boots was asleep in front of the fire. He woke, stretched right up to the table on his big back legs, licked Joe's face with his sandpaper tongue, and vanished. Joe searched and called but he was nowhere to be found.

When he asked his mother about him, she said she'd never seen the cat, either at the farm or the flat.

Joe never saw him again.

Only, sometimes, when things grew difficult or he was unhappy, it would seem that he would feel the fleeting rasp of a sandpaper tongue on his hand and the flourish of a bushy tail around his legs.

M13 and the Nine Days' Wonder

told by X, who doesn't dare to give his name.
Well, would you if you wrote something like this?

If you are at all squeamish by nature, leave out this story. You have been warned.

Mandy the Boot came in looking like a water buffalo deprived of its water hole, and said through her missing front tooth—she hasn't had it fixed yet since she was in that fight with Killer Wales last week, and lost the fight and the tooth—that owing to the fact that Slasher Ormeroyd had broken the school rules (and ours) about knives, our class would be the only one not going on the school trip next week. The school rule is don't bring knives to school, ours is don't get found out if you do.

Killer Wales looked up from his Lego at this bit of information and made one of his three noises. The first means he is happy. That doesn't happen very often. The second means he is not happy. And that doesn't happen very often. The third means he is angry and will duff up the nearest person if they don't watch out. This last happens nearly all the time and is how he came to have that scrap with Mandy the Boot. And it was the third noise he made just then, at the beginning of Monday morning, giving me the idea that it was not going to be an easy sort of week, not that ours often are. Not with M13.

Killer Wales is six foot two and growing nicely though it should take him till late teens to reach eight foot.

But just as I was awaiting with some curiosity the outcome of a scrap between Killer and Slasher, for they've never really sorted it out in their long battle-torn progress up the school, Felix the Cat looked up from his game of poker with Lia Tansy, Tom Lightfinger and Chinky Fred to indicate that this was not just Killer's business alone, but a matter that should be brought before the whole of M13, and instructed us all to meet behind the cycle shed at 11.50 a.m. Such is the power of the Cat that we all arrived, though Brain Drain was late, not knowing what 11.50 was, and Hag Stevens because she'd pinched a small one's lunch in passing. By then, Abdullah the Libyan was sharing his doughnuts before settling to a snog with Maybelle, Mandy the Boot was separating Asra and the Heap, who hate each other, and Tom Lightfinger was handing out fags and roll-ups to those with the necessary cash.

Slasher was in the doghouse, of course, and this made it a bit tricky, for Slasher usually conducts the meetings, as the Cat never does anything that might tire him; he likes to keep his powers in reserve. Somebody then offered me the job, no way, I said, but many thanks for the compliment etc.

"What about Women's Lib.?" snarled Mandy the Boot through her tobacco-chewing.

"Right, then, you do it," pronounced the Cat.

"On behalf of our Chairperson here," began Mandy, "one Felix Delaney known as the Cat, I should like to

84

draw the attention of M13 to the crime of one Peter Ormeroyd, known as Slasher, to wit ..."

"Tu-whoo, to-whoo," warbled Dizzy. He'd been strangely quiet all morning. One of his nutty sessions coming on, probably. It was about due.

"Shut up," growled Killer.

"You put me off," complained Mandy, then continued, "being found in possession of one sheath knife, as a result of which the entire class is to be punished by being deprived of its annual school trip, a highlight of the year."

"Jolly good, Boot," applauded Bat Pearson.

"The question now before us, M13, is what are we going to do about this?"

"Kill 'im," said Killer, simply.

"Send him to Coventry, man," put in Hot Chocolate, one of the more trustworthy and old-fashioned members of the class (as a result of reading all the Famous Five books).

"Vot's dis plice, Coventry, gawt to do wiv it? Diss ain't Coventry," asked Brain Drain, painfully.

Mandy the Boot was wearing the bad-tempered look for which she is famed throughout the school.

"It means nobody speaks to him at all," she snapped.

"Nobody much speaks to me, anyway," said Slasher.

"That's cos you're horrible," explained Killer.

"If we're stuck in school working when everyone else is out on a trip, who cares whether we speak or not? We shall be too fed up to care," commented Tom.

"Work? We never *work*," said Hag Stevens.

"Too true. We hear this said all the time," added the Heap. Asra spat reflectively.

"But I really wanted to find out if the cave is palaeolithic or mesolithic," moaned Bat, "and I was looking forward to the stalactites and stalagmites even if they are said to be overrated."

The school trip was to a famous prehistoric cave and museum.

"'ark at 'er. Sure you'me got them words right, Bat?" asked Brain Drain.

"I am almost invariably correct, despite the fact that I am hampered, according to the experts, by the fact of being in with you lot in a mixed ability class and insufficiently stretched. But I don't mind. Who needs stretching when I got you, Killer?"

Killer smiled soppily. "If yer wants to be stretched, Bat, I'll put yer on a rack any time."

He loves Bat because she does all his work for him; on his report he got "inarticulate in class, but surprisingly good written work". This pleased him, though he couldn't actually read it, of course, but Bat spelt it out for him. We've read all our end-of-term reports. The Cat unlocked the filing cabinet in the secretary's office with a bit of bent wire. A student, poor thing, had made the comment, "His spelling is week," on the Cat's, which of course made him very happy, he claimed he blackmailed him out of a fiver to keep quiet and alter it. And at this point, the Cat, who had been sitting quietly, spoke abruptly to Mandy. She banged her feet in her father's size 12 army boots.

"Come on. We're wasting time. What are we gonna do about Slasher being found with a knife and the school trip cancelled?"

"Bloomin' Slasher's bin found with a bloomin' knife

since he was in nappies," Killer muttered.

"We know that. Come on, everybody. Some suggestions. And not that sort."

"I know," put in Lia Tansy, from her seat beside the Cat, her golden eyes very wide, "we'll be good, for … for … nine days. Yes, for nine days. That's how long we've got to the trip."

"Crazy."

"Mad."

"Load o' rubbish."

"No way."

"Can't be done."

"You've gone nutty, Lia."

End of play whistle blew.

"I like it," said the Cat. "It's on."

"End of meeting," shouted the Boot. "Daisy Chain, you can inform Sir. Slasher, you can clear up."

Mr. Perkins, sir, is fond of Daisy Chain. She's lovable, like Paddington Bear, and there aren't many like that in M13. He came in, sighing, as he often does when he comes in to us. He's a nice man, Mr. Perkins, but life had reduced him to a fair state of misery, especially a life that includes us when he's nearing the end of it. We've got a fund going for a wreath in case being with us too much gives him a heart attack before he reaches retirement, only Lightfinger keeps dipping into it to pay his gambling debts.

"BBC Singing Together," began Mr. Perkins, "and then Maths Today," he added, shuddering, "and the Lord have mercy on us."

Daisy got up at a nod from the Cat.

"Please, sir," she said, and for a minute his wrinkles lifted, for she's a very pretty girl with her golden hair and blue eyes and off-the-shoulder blouse and long skirt given to her by her sister who's twice as big as Daisy. They keep floating off her. Then her lovely eyes went blank. Daisy had forgotten again.

"School trip," Bat prompted.

"Oh yes. Mr. Perkins. What do you think? We're going to be good."

"What horrible news," he replied, sitting down suddenly. "You've made me feel quite ill."

Brain Drain, whose job it is, for everyone tries to keep him usefully occupied, turned on the radio, and the jolly but incomprehensible sounds of "Weel May The Keel Raw" bellowed through the room at maximum volume.

"Open your pamphlets, and we'll tackle this bravely, together," roared Mr. Perkins, above the din. M13 is not a musical class. We rawed the keel in our different ways, Killer making the noise of Early Man pursued by Tyrannosaurus Rex, and Slasher trying out a punk rock version. Mandy was on Disco.

Eventually it ended, though Dizzy continued on a high gibbering note for some time. He was definitely due for one of his funnies.

"Please, Mr. Perkins," Daisy began again. "We want to go on our school trip."

Mandy, impatient, went on. "Slasher is sorry about the knife. We'll be good for nine days, if you'll let us. Besides, Bat wants to see the stalactites and stalagmites."

88

"WE ALL WANT THE STALACTITES AND STALAGMITES."

Killer managed smagglemites nicely. Brain Drain just opened and closed his mouth.

"Well," said Mr. Perkins. "Little did I think that I should ever hear M13 regretting the error of its ways. However, as it happens, it is right out of my hands and in those of your Head-teacher, Mr. Bliss."

We thought about that in silence. This was not going to be easy. Mr. Bliss does not live up to his name.

"Let Slasher stay at school, while we go."

Mr. Perkins held up a hand. "I feel you should know that Mr. Bliss decided on this not only because of the knife but also because of the general standard of behaviour throughout the year."

"Not fair. We paid our money."

"Well, I must admit that the thought of *not* having to appear with you in public in one of your livelier moods makes me quite happy to return it to you. Apart from that which Tom has er, nicked."

"I didn't know you knew, sir!"

"Of course I know. I know if a plastic penny disappears from the Infants' Shop. It'll just be you keeping your hand in."

"I'm not that bad, sir!"

"No. Worse."

Felix the Cat decided to interrupt.

"We're not getting anywhere, sir."

"Couldn't we do something as well as being good? Something positive," put in Bat.

"Such as?"

"Looking after the Infants at play-time, and playing with them?"

"I don't think you really appreciate your reputation in this school. They'd be terrified."

"Running an anti-litter campaign?"

"A very successful one is being run already by M9 and M10. Or hadn't you noticed?"

"Patrolling the toilets," suggested Killer hopefully.

Mr. Perkins shuddered. "With you outside, most of the lower school wouldn't ever go, Wales."

"I know," said the Cat, dreamily. "We'll clear the rest of the school bomb site."

During the war a bomb had fallen, not on the school, unfortunately, but on the school house. No one was hurt, but the house was completely flattened, though the school was undamaged, apart from broken windows etc. Afterwards many schemes were thought up about what should be done with it. These all came to the same thing. Nothing.

So in our day, the bomb site was covered with brambles, bushes, nettles, wild flowers, tins, cartons, aerosol cans, old rusty wire, old clothes, and a corrugated iron hut in a jungle corner where one end of the school meets a street of terrace houses known as Paradise Row.

And, like victims, we were being offered up by the Cat to clear it. And no one would argue. Killer and Slasher *look* dangerous. But you don't argue with the Cat.

Operations began that day.

Wellies, gloves, old shirts, overalls, hats, all from Lost Property, were provided, together with spades, shovels, forks and other implements, all to be checked daily by Hot Chocolate. Large polythene bags awaited the rubbish.

And RULES FOR THE NINE DAYS was pinned to the class notice board.

1. No bad language even under extreme provocation.

2. No fighting, kicking, spitting, rowdy arguing, or quarrelling, even under provocation.

3. No stealing, not even from other classes.

4. No bullying, not even of other classes.

5. Work to be done to the best of one's ability and handed in on time.

6. No groping or snogging in public.

7. All rooms and resources to be left tidy at the end of each day.

8. Full attendance at all classes, including Assemblies, PE and Games.

9. All members of the class to be neatly and conventionally dressed. No safety pins, newly dyed hair, freaky jewellery, make-up or weapons.

10. No sweets, coke, fish and chips, chewing gum, cigarettes, alcohol or sausages in school.

Tom Lightfinger was almost in tears by the time he finished reading it out loud to Killer and Brain Drain, and then the Cat had to be fetched to stop Killer tearing Slasher to pieces. Several of the class were not speaking to Slasher.

Only the Cat could have got us through that Nine Days. His cold eyes, his mean disposition helped us when we would have weakened.

News ran like lightning through the school. Bets were

laid as to whether we could see them through or not, the opinion generally being *not*. Other sneaks, creeps, and weasels were taking advantage of the rules to harass us.

And we didn't need harassing. Clearing the bomb site was horrible, hard, dirty and tough. Nettles stung us, brambles tore us, the ground was stony and cruel; creepy crawlies, spiders, earwigs, slugs, centipedes and snails lurked everywhere. We grew tired, jumpy. Dizzy was zonked up like an overstretched spring. Every play-time and lunch-hour, and after school, we toiled and sweated, while in lessons, old Perkins, smiling at last, piled exercise on exercise, work card on work card, test on test, essay on essay. Some people finished an exercise book for the first time ever.

Gone were the happy days behind the shed with supplies and snogging. And the strain began to tell. Bat, working for two, was white with red-rimmed eyes. Abdullah and Maybelle quarrelled, and he cried, saying she only wanted him for his doughnuts. Asra and the Heap grew very nasty with everyone else as they couldn't get at each other. Tom Lightfinger, a crazed look in his eyes, was found walking round the supermarket with hands sellotaped together to stop him shoplifting.

"It's hard to stop doing something you've been at since you were three," he moaned as Hag Stevens led him home.

But there were good times. Killer tearing down the iron hut, so that we could jump it to little bits; Dizzy discovering an ancient pair of bloomers and doing a happy dance in them till Rule 9 was remembered. The sun shone. Mr. Perkins kept on smiling. Parents came to school to find out why their children were going straight to bed after tea and sleeping like logs.

The verdict was to be announced by Mr. Bliss, on Thursday afternoon. But by lunch-time M13 was nearly finished, exhausted, as the temperature sailed up into the nineties.

"I didn't want to go, anyway," moaned Killer, working on the thistles in the final corner. "I hate school trips. Bl . . ."

"Belt up," snarled the Cat, thin and mean with fatigue, sunglasses black on his white face.

Slasher was snivelling and dribbling.

"I hate myself," he whimpered.

"We hate yourself, as well," we answered.

"Don't anyone go on with this for my sake," whispered Bat. "I'll go in the holidays."

Into the misery, the Cat spat poison.

"Just see what I do to the person who gives up now. They'd only look for a quicker way to die."

We pressed on.

"I've just struck sommat in this mound thing," Killer grunted. "There. It's quite deep down, but it's sommat all right."

"Treasure?" asked Tom. He was cheered up.

So was Bat.

"Mound, did you say, Killer? Here, let me look."

"There's some old cracked pot here," went on Killer. "An' looks like some bones and stuff."

But Bat was shrieking and dancing about.

"Hold it, Killer, hold it. Don't dig any more. We must leave it for the experts. Oh, look, look. Oh, Killer,

I love you. Give it to me. Oh, Killer! Everybody! I think it's Urn Burial!"

"Eh?" said Killer.

"Bronze Age. Even better than the cave. And here in our school. This must be an old religious site!"

"That doesn't surprise me at all," said the Cat.

At that moment the whistle blew for afternoon school, and as M13 gathered itself wearily together, Daisy Chain tottered sleepily out of a hole just below the back walls of Paradise Row, where she'd been cheating and having a little zizz.

"I got somefink, too," she crooned to whatever she was holding in her arms, an earth-caked cylinder-shaped thing with fins on it.

The Cat is quick—you can say that for him.

"My God," he yelled, rules about language forgotten, "Daisy, Daisy, give it to Killer, he's the fastest, and *Killer, run like hell as far as the school gate and dump it, fast. Fast! Git! And the rest of you, lie down! Lie down, you load of morons! Drop dead! Or you will be!*"

And he was already flat in a hollow, hands over ears.

I could only think, as I fell down too, that heat and work had sent the Cat bananas, and we'd better tell old Perkins as soon as poss., when CRRRUUUMMMPP exploded at the school gate, filling the air with dust, gravel and bits of flying cars. Getting to my feet, I saw the school secretary, followed closely by Mr. Bliss and other people, rush out of the front door. But above all the confusion, two things stuck in my mind—one, Bat, still standing, her face ecstatic, clutching a large broken flower-pot, and the blackened form of Killer, clothes in shreds, lurching erratically towards us.

94

"What did I ever do to you?" he cried, and then, "What did you do to *that*?" He waved an arm at the chaos behind him and collapsed at the feet of the Cat.

The school trip was cancelled.

Police were investigating bomb damage, the residents of Paradise Row were repairing house damage, the Staff were organising their car insurance, and M13 were sleeping.

A while later, on a radiant afternoon, the school filed into the Hall, where upon the platform sat the Bishop, the Mayor, the School Managers, and the President of the Archaeological Society. Just below the platform, in a position of honour, sat M13, the more fidgety and unstable ones, such as Dizzy, placed where they could be thumped or kicked quietly. Neat clothing was to be seen, and such hair as was blue or pink had been cut very short.

After introductions, the President of the Archaeological Society spoke. It was a woman, Mandy the Boot noted approvingly. She said:

"In this world of today, when we so often hear the youth of this country criticised for its behaviour or lack of interest in education, it gives me especial pleasure to praise this class, this fine body of children that we see before us here, children who have worked so hard, and made so exciting a discovery, the finest Bronze Age burial barrow so far found in this region, and possibly leading to even finer discoveries if we are permitted to continue the dig around the school. In this wonderful urn, an excellent specimen indeed, was found the remains of a child sacrificed on this site centuries ago, and rediscovered by sacrifice again, the sacrifice of these truly remarkable children of Class M . . . er . . . er . . . 13. Moreover, the erudition and scholarship shown by one of them, er . . . er . . . Beatrice Pearson, has led me to think that some of the finest education in this country must be going on here, in this school.

"The finds are to be presented to the Museum, where a plaque will be inscribed to the class, M . . . er . . . er . . . 13. And now I should like to present each member of the class with a small cheque in token of our appreciation of their achievement."

Amid loud applause M13 lurched to collect its booty. The Chairman of the Managers rose to his feet.

"But that is not all," he said. "This class does not only possess brains and the will to work, it possesses great courage as well. And in recognition of that fact, here we have the Mayor to present further tokens of appreciation from the residents of Paradise Row, who, according to the Police Report, have been at terrible risk from an unexploded bomb ever since the war. First we should like to honour Eric Wales, who, to save his friends, ran with this deadly bomb and saved the day, putting himself in danger, regardless of his own safety."

Killer lumbered up to the platform and bent over the Mayor to receive a medal. As the rest of us filed up to collect our tokens of appreciation, we were pleased to note that these were postal orders, easier for ready cash, hissed Tom out of the corner of his mouth on the way back. Then we stood up to sing the school song, "With glad hearts serving others." M13 sang with great enthusiasm, if little tune.

Behind the cycle shed all was bliss, no, not Mr. Bliss. Doughnuts and chocolates, fags, cider, ice-cream, coke, were being handed out in huge quantities, thanks to the P.O.s. Abdullah was snogging with Maybelle, Asra and the Heap were at it again. Chinky Fred was organising a game of poker, Bat was telling Killer about the Beaker people, and the Cat was chatting up a new girl with long black hair and green eyes, watched by Lia out of cold golden ones, as she fingered a knife in her high suede boots. . . . Tom was equally quietly picking the pocket of an unfortunate new boy.

"Only the exams left to worry about now," said the Boot.

The Cat looked up. "Oh, don't give them a thought. I've photocopied all the test papers and Bat's working on them at the weekend. Just relax and enjoy yourselves."

So we did. M13 relaxed and enjoyed itself, for it always obeyed the Cat.

Crasher

A June afternoon, hot, sunny; a thatched country house, flowers and green lawns, looking like the set for a TV series, with people in jodhpurs, or long dresses and floppy hats, or purple tweed skirts with stick-out bottoms; loud English county voices talking about meets and hands, and other things often incomprehensible to Meg. Her voice was quite different, she knew, for she had heard it on tape back in Birmingham, where they lived before. Tim, her brother, had a different voice, too. She turned and grinned at him, but most of his face was lost behind an enormous ice-cream.

People started to talk in even louder tones. Something was about to happen at last. The judges were coming to a decision. The hound pack inside its fence moved in ever-changing circles. People inspected them from time to time, singling out a hound for special attention.

"Which one was ours?" asked Tim. "I can't tell. They all look alike. And they have black patches. Crasher was all white and tan."

"That happens with foxhounds. The black comes as they grow older."

"Seems a funny thing to do."

"I know. But that's what they told me. Though it seems queer not to be able to recognise an animal you had in the house for ages."

"Look, they've pulled out the winner."

Over the tannoy came an announcement.

"We are pleased to announce the winner. Stentor Rushford-Barton has been unanimously chosen as the finest foxhound of the year. He was bred by Mrs. Humphries-Haynes of Challacombe Stitch, and reared by Mrs. Gittings of Murchington Farm. Will those ladies come forward to receive their trophies, please?"

Tim pushed Meg forward.

"Congrats, my dear," bellowed a lady, pumping her hand up and down.

"Mrs. Gittings?" asked the chairman.

"Oh, no, not me. My mother couldn't come," answered Meg.

"Then you shall receive the prize. Congratulations on a very fine dog. You've done quite a good job, there."

Once more Meg's hand was pumped up and down, and a huge silver cup with purple ribbons on its handles was given to her. It was heavy, so she put it on the lawn as she bent down to pat the very fine dog in question. He yawned widely as the crowd clapped. Would he know her, wondered Meg? Would he remember her? It was quite a while since he was taken back to the kennels. If it came to that, did she know him? He didn't at all resemble the Crasher she'd known, not this big animal called Stentor Rushford-Barton. Mind you, he'd got enormous great feet . . . that was how he'd first got the name Crasher.

She whispered into the nearest ear, "Crasher . . . Crasher . . . Bumblefoot."

The ear twitched and he looked up at her.

Her aunt Dinah had brought the puppy home one Saturday evening and put him on a mat in the kitchen, where he sat, legs splayed out, a lost, bewildered white-and-tan heap. The Master of the Hounds had given him to her, for he was busy pursuing her at the time. Meg's Aunt Dinah was young and the sort of girl who had lots of men pursuing her.

"What's that doing there, then?" asked Meg's mum, hands on hips. She was rather like a bulldozer, and did not have lots of people pursuing her, only Dad, who was in the Navy, leaving Mum and Meg at home with Tim, aged seven, and Moggy, aged one, nearly.

"If we look after him for six months, we stand a chance of winning a prize," explained Aunt Dinah.

"You must be joking. We've already got two dogs, a cat, five puppies, four kittens and a tortoise."

Meg's mum was always acquiring animals, but trying not to. She was trying hard not to right now.

"You mean to tell me that they have the colossal cheek to expect us to feed that for nothing? For six whole months? No, Dinah, no. For it will grow, mark my words, you can tell by the size of its paws. That dog will be enormous. Besides, I will not have a foxhound in this house. You know very well what I think of fox-hunting."

"If you hate it that much, then why did you come here? You knew it was hunting country."

"I came because the countryside is beautiful and I wanted to paint it, not watch people galloping around killing things. And, another thing, Dinah, it won't be you looking after that animal, it will be me, won't it? You've never looked after a thing in your life."

One of the things about Meg's mother was that she was a great believer in coming out with the truth, and sometimes this could be like living with a piece of sandpaper. You got rubbed raw. But Dinah wasn't bothered. Nothing worried her for long. The two dogs were sniffing at the puppy. Both being female, they cared for it and wagged their tails. Tim liked it as well, curling up on the mat beside it, but Meg watched and waited. She didn't intend committing herself to liking it unless it was going to stay.

Aunt Dinah grinned. "I'd have thought you'd have wanted to do something to oblige the county. Just think of the honour."

"You cheeky so and so," replied Meg's mum, but she was laughing. Whenever Dinah made her angry, she made her laugh again afterwards, and it would all be all right. And then the puppy lurched out of its circle of admirers and somehow half fell, half tottered over to Meg's mum, put out its tongue and licked her toes, bare in their sandals, and fell fast asleep on her foot. Meg relaxed. It was all settled now. Her mother dropped down beside it, carefully keeping the foot still.

"You poor, tired thing. You're worn out. You can't help what people make you do, can you?" She rubbed her face against its coat. "You smell warm and biscuity."

Aunt Dinah grinned at Meg. She'd got her way. But then, she always did.

"Mind you," said Mrs. Gittings, "you're all going to help look after it and train it."

Right from the first, he turned out to be a dreadful dog, greedy, a bully and a coward.

He grew fast and as he grew he started to bully the other animals, especially the small ones. He couldn't scare Ruby, the mongrel, who was as fast and clever as a fox, but he bullied the puppies and Aunt Dinah's little poodle, rolling his great haunches over them and sending them flying. He was difficult to train and made messes everywhere, annoying the cat, a very fastidious animal. And he finished off the tortoise. One day it stretched out its neck too far and Crasher bit it off. Tim laughed for hours over that.

"You've got a horrible sense of humour," Meg said coldly, walking away from him. She refused to speak to him for a week.

And still Crasher grew. Larger, but, more especially, heavier. At night he slept in one of the sheds, but Mrs. Gittings used to let him in early when she fed Moggy. Then Crasher would thunder down the passage on his great feet, up the stairs, knock open the door, fling himself on Meg's bed, hold her down by both ears and lick her face thoroughly, beginning with the nose. Meg was not a big girl and it was almost impossible to move for about ten minutes. So she took to early rising, getting out of bed before the dawn thundered up in the shape of Crasher. The noise he made with his feet got him the name of Bumblefoot.

Moggy's birthday arrived, and there was to be a super tea with huge cake. Whether Moggy, now aged one year, would appreciate all this, they didn't know, but Meg and Tim looked forward to it. Meg placed the cake in the middle of the table, stood back to admire it and went to fetch the other goodies, ham, salad, jelly, cream. She arrived back to no cake, and Crasher swallowing gulpily. Meg was furious, but in the straight race that followed Crasher beat her through the front door and across the fields. It was

particularly sad because they only got cakes like that when Meg's Mum's painting was going badly—for then she cleaned the house frantically, banging carpets, polishing, baking for a siege, it seemed. Then her painting would start again, and they'd be back to baked beans and dust everywhere. They didn't mind.

Autumn set in, with falling leaves and misty nights. At the farm, they settled in for a quiet winter. The children were not often left alone, but one evening Moggy had to be taken for an injection, and Dinah was away. The house was quiet, the nearest neighbour more than a mile from them. Suddenly, Ruby tensed and leapt up on the sofa beneath the window. The poodle joined her and they began to bark. Something was wandering about in the dark outside. Meg was not usually alarmed but, as she looked out of the window at the misty swirls outside, she didn't feel at all happy.

"Have a look out of the kitchen door," suggested Tim.

"No way," she replied. "It just might be the Hound of the Baskervilles out there."

"I'll creep round and check all the doors," whispered Tim, "and you get all the dogs together to frighten it off."

All the dogs? Where was the other one? She set off in search of their biggest animal. It took her a time to discover him, but she managed it in the end. Lying stiff under the bed, paws over ears, tail lying flat, trembling piteously, lay Crasher, looking after himself, if not the home. She tried to drag him back with her, for she could not carry him, but he lay limp. Eventually she tried to get him on to the sofa to help with the barking, but it was no use, he crawled under it instead. Still, Ruby, at last, gave a satisfied flourish of her tail, that indicated she had done her duty properly, and descended from her perch to seek her supper. Whatever had been around had disappeared into the night.

"Come on, then, you great coward," Meg said to Crasher, handing out the food dishes to them all, whereupon he walloped down the kittens' share just to show how big and strong he was. Meg smacked his rear end but he didn't seem to feel anything at all, he was so well covered by now.

And still he grew. Dinah never took him for walks, though she patted his head at times and gave him an unsuitable tit-bit. But Tim and Meg roamed for miles with the dogs. One day they were crossing a field, a very steep field, such as you get in that part of the world, looking as if it's almost standing on end, with a bramble-filled hollow set in the centre. On the other side of the drystone wall a wood descended steeply to the road. And suddenly, without their having noticed, Meg, Tim and the dogs were surrounded by a herd of bullocks. Meg knew that bullocks take little interest in people but a great deal in dogs, and calling out, "Come on," she headed for a stile in the wall, leading into the wood. Ruby shot ahead like a greyhound, the rest tumbling after, falling and rolling, over the stile and down between the scrub oak and the beeches to the road below, where Meg dusted them over and sorted them out on the grass bank.

There was no Crasher.

"That dratted dog," Tim said. "He's still up there, somewhere."

They peered over the wall. No sign of the foxhound, but the bullocks were circling the bramble hollow in a very moody fashion, lowering their horns and stamping. All tales about how completely harmless they are seemed unconvincing to Meg at that moment.

"He's in that thicket," she said.

"I'll fetch him," Tim said. Meg looked at him. Tim was seven and not very big. "No, I'll go. You hold these two."

Back she climbed up the hill, not at all happy. There, ringed round the bramble bushes, the bullocks moved restlessly. Right in the centre, in a little clearing, head down, paws over ears, trembling again, lay the sturdy form of Crasher. Meg climbed over the brambles and, using strength she didn't know she had, she picked him up, making her way through the thorns, knees giving a bit with the weight, and praying as she went. And there was Tim, the other two dogs tethered tight to him, shouting at the bullocks, shooing them away, and telling them generally what he thought about them. And they went. Slowly they wheeled and trotted off across the field to the other side.

The little band made its way home, extremely slowly on account of the fact that Meg had to carry Crasher, since every time he was placed on the ground his legs gave way again. By the time they were almost there, she fell in a heap on the bank, saying she couldn't go any further. Ruby, obviously dying to get a move on, looked at them, then nipped Crasher smartly on his rear end where he was sitting. After that he managed to walk the rest of the way.

The next day he stole a joint of meat out of the fridge,

when Mrs. Gittings had opened the door and turned her back for a moment only.

"I shall be glad when that animal's gone," she exclaimed.

Everyone agreed.

They came to collect him at last. A man with a van arrived one day.

"Where's the hound? Stentor Rushford?" he said.

That was indeed the question. Crasher was nowhere to be seen. Calling brought Ruby and the poodle but no hound.

But Meg knew where he would be, and he was. Crasher, the coward, was under her bed, paws over ears, trembling, trying to be a little little dog, hiding. She tried to pull him out, told him not to be afraid, that everything would be all right, that he would like the kennels, that he wouldn't miss Tim and her and Mum, and the dogs and taking the kittens' food, but it was no good. He wouldn't stir. So she crawled under the bed with him and cried. Quite soon Tim joined them. There, their mother found them.

"You can have him for one more week," said the man with the van.

One morning during that week Meg woke very, very early, and fetched Crasher out of the shed before he thundered up the dawn. As they went through the gate into the fields Tim appeared and slipped quietly along beside them. They didn't say anything, just ran through the cool morning mist up the hill to the start of the moor. Over the short grass and the heather they ran on until Meg cried, "Oh, stop," and they crouched low and still while Meg grabbed the hound by its collar. There ahead of them, across a hill strewn with boulders, appeared a large fox, nose down, brush up in the air, running lightly through the morning.

"Keep still," whispered Meg. Crasher watched with them, as it loped on and disappeared into the trees. Then they, too, turned for home.

"It was very big," said Tim.

"A dog fox," Meg replied.

At breakfast Crasher drank the kittens' milk and got smacked.

Two days later the man in the van returned, and this time Crasher left, wagging his tail a little, not afraid. Meg didn't cry, only a bit in bed that night.

The ear twitched and he looked at her, a large and handsome dog. She could hear her father saying:

"Hound dogs are just about the most stupid dogs there are, for they have only the intelligence of the pack."

Meg thought he was probably right. Then Crasher wagged his tail and a warm tongue slid over her face.

"Don't forget to lead them *away* from the foxes," she whispered, and turned to go.

MAN IN MOTION
Jan Mark

Once Lloyd has started at his new school, he soon finds he's playing cricket with Salman, swimming with Kenneth, cycling with James and playing badminton with Vlad. But American football is Lloyd's greatest enthusiasm. And in time it tests his loyalties, not only to his other sporting activities, but also to the new friends he shares them with.

THE OUTSIDE CHILD
Nina Bawden

Imagine suddenly discovering you have a step-brother and -sister no one has ever told you about! It's the most exciting thing that's ever happened to Jane, and she can't wait to meet them. Perhaps at last she will become part of a 'proper' family, instead of for ever being the outside child. So begins a long search for her brother and sister, but when she finally does track them down, Jane finds there are still more surprises in store!

THE FOX OF SKELLAND
Rachel Dixon

Samantha's never liked the old custom of Foxing Day – the fox costume especially gives her the creeps. So when Jason and Rib, children of the new publicans at The Fox and Lady, find the costume and Jason wears it to the fancy-dress disco, she's sure something awful will happen.

Then Sam's old friend Joseph sees the ghost of the Lady and her fox. Has she really come back to exact vengeance on the village? Or has her appearance got something to do with the spate of burglaries in the area?